A Hug From Daddy

A Novel

Obieray Rogers

Cover: Dynamic Creative Solutions (www.dynamiccreativesolutions.com)
Editing: Kritike Editorial Services (www.kritike-edit.com)

ISBN 978-0-9764022-2-0

Powerful Purpose Publishing Company
P O Box 32132, Columbus, OH 43232

Printed in the United States of America.

This book is dedicated with love to all who brought this work to being. I could not have produced this without your help, support, prayers and encouragement. Thank you.

Psalm 91 – The Message

You, who sit down in the High God's presence, spend the night in Shaddai's shadow say this: "God, you're my refuge. I trust in you and I'm safe!" That's right—He rescues you from hidden traps, shields you from deadly hazards. His huge outstretched arms protect you—under them you're perfectly safe; His arms fend off all harm. Fear nothing—not wild wolves in the night, not flying arrows in the day, not disease that prowls through the darkness, not disaster that erupts at high noon. Even though others succumb all around, drop like flies right and left, no harm will even graze you. You'll stand untouched, watch it all from a distance, watch the wicked turn into corpses. Yes, because God is your refuge, the High God your very own home, evil can't get close to you, harm can't get through the door. He ordered His angels to guard you wherever you go. If you stumble, they'll catch you; their job is to keep you from falling. You'll walk unharmed among lions and snakes, and kick your lions and serpents from the path. "If you'll hold on to me for dear life," says God, "I'll get you out of any trouble. I'll give you the best of care if you'll only get to know and trust me. Call me and I'll answer, be at your side in bad times; I'll rescue you, then throw you a party. I'll give you long life, give you a long drink of salvation."

CHAPTER ONE

THIS YEAR —NEW YEAR'S EVE—EARLY MORNING
COLUMBUS, OHIO

Michelle Nickelson Stephens didn't necessarily believe in premonitions. She did believe there were times when you just felt that something was going to happen and then it did. Today was one of those times. She couldn't put her finger on it and wouldn't have been able to explain how she knew what she knew. She just did. And she knew that whatever was about to happen would be both mind-boggling and life-changing.

Michelle believed that every day was a blank canvas and that everything that happened—whether good or bad—was merely the brush strokes of the masterpiece called life. As far as she was concerned, that meant whatever happened was supposed to happen. She could go along with whatever God had planned or she could kick, scream and resist and still end up going along with whatever God had planned. Michelle did not feel like kicking and screaming today. As a matter of fact, she was excited about whatever was getting ready to happen. She reflected back to those times when the day started out one way and ended another. Or the way someone would bless her just out of the blue. Or…

"Yikes!" Michelle was surprised by the unexpected burst of cold water and scrambled to turn it off. She exited the shower shivering and grabbed a bath sheet off the rack. That's what you get for daydreaming, she thought.

Michelle used a portion of the towel to wipe the steam off the mirror and leaned in closer. She was fortunate to have good clear skin, the color of peanut butter, and unlike a lot of her friends, she never had a problem with acne. She frowned slightly as she touched the scar just above her naturally arched left eyebrow, which was the only flaw in an otherwise flawless complexion. She had long curly hair, eyes so dark they appeared black and full lips. She was a pretty woman.

She removed her hair clip and used her fingers to try to bring order to the chaos of curls surrounding her heart-shaped face. Her husband, Michael, loved her hair and jokingly threatened divorce if she ever cut it. Although she was grateful for the thickness and length, sometimes long hair was just a pain to take care of so she wore her hair up during the day, but at night she took it down for her man. Tangled hair was a small price to pay for the look in Michael's eyes when he played with her hair.

"Hey, babe," Michael called through the door. "Breakfast is almost ready."

"I'll be right out." Michelle removed the towel and looked at herself in the full-length mirror. At age thirty-one she still looked good although she was carrying an extra twenty pounds. Michael assured her that he loved every inch of her. She blushed as she remembered her husband's demonstration of appreciation earlier this morning.

Michelle slipped on the robe hanging on the door and walked into the bedroom. She could smell the specialty-blended coffee Michael preferred. They had made a commitment when they married to have at least one meal together every day. Breakfast was their time. No newspapers, telephones or televisions were allowed to interfere.

The table was already set when Michelle walked into the sitting area. Michael was pouring coffee and had his back turned. She liked the way her husband looked. He was seven inches taller than her five foot eight and was a muscular two hundred and fifteen pounds. He played football in high school and still kept in shape. His skin was the color of a dark chocolate candy bar. He was clean shaven, except for a goatee that framed his full lips, with straight white teeth and dimples. He possessed a voice that was smooth as silk and one that still made her stomach flutter every time she heard it.

Michelle walked up behind Michael and ran her hands over his flat stomach. "Everything looks good." Michelle stretched to kiss his ear. Michael loved to cook and could create a feast with just a few ingredients. Michelle never knew whether they would have cold cereal and

2

fruit or eggs Benedict. Breakfast was always a surprise and always delicious. Today the table was piled with grits, scrambled eggs, bacon and fruit. This was definitely not a cold cereal day.

"Thanks honey." Michael bent down to kiss Michelle softly on the mouth. "Good morning again beautiful."

"Well, aren't you the smooth talker."

"Just calling it like I see it, babe. Come and sit down before breakfast gets cold." Michael seated Michelle and fingered the sleeve of her robe. "This looks good on you."

"Is that why you bought it?" Michelle coyly asked. The robe was a peach-colored silk that was just one of the many gifts Michael gave her for Christmas.

"I knew it was you." Michael winked as he took his seat across from Michelle.

"Judging by the way you're looking at me, I might need to wear it more often."

"It doesn't matter what you wear. The reaction will be the same."

Michelle smiled softly in response. "Thank you."

"My pleasure," Michael smiled in return, causing his dimples to deepen. He knew exactly the effect he had on his wife because she stirred him the same way. "Let's bless the food before I forget all the things I need to do today."

After saying amen, Michelle handed Michael a glass of orange juice. "What time will you be home?"

"No later than seven." Michael was traveling to Cleveland to see a client and Michelle knew he would also stop in to see his father, Donavon. Both Michael and Michelle had been raised in Cleveland, Ohio and Michael's father still lived in Shaker Heights. "The paper said we're not expected to have snow until late evening so the roads should be clear. This will be our first New Year's Eve, babe. There's no way I'm not spending it with you," Michael grinned at Michelle. "What's on your agenda for today?"

"I'm going to the office for a few hours. Maybe without so many interruptions, I'll get some work done."

"Are you going to make it home before the snow starts?"

"I should be home by four-thirty. Is there anything special you want for dinner?"

"Just you, baby."

"You're a mess."

"Yeah, but you love me." Michael grabbed his suit jacket off the hanger. "Come on and walk me to the door. I need to hit the road."

Linking hands, they walked through the house to the garage. Once there Michael slipped his arms around Michelle. "Lord, this is a day that you have made so we'll rejoice and be glad in it. Watch over us throughout this day and continue to keep us in the palm of your hand. Grant traveling mercies to us as we go and bring us back together at the appointed time. In Jesus' name we pray. Amen."

"Amen," Michelle responded and kissed Michael. "Love you. See you tonight."

"Love you, too."

CHAPTER TWO

NEW YEAR'S EVE—LATE AFTERNOON

Being caught in bumper to bumper traffic was not in my plans, Michelle thought, although she shouldn't have been surprised. Her morning's devotional reading was about patience and what better way to learn that than sitting in traffic? All she wanted was to get home, fix a cup of hot chocolate and soak in the Jacuzzi.

Michelle turned into her housing complex and hit the garage door opener as she approached the circular driveway. She dropped everything—coat, purse, briefcase and cell phone—on the kitchen counter and headed straight for her bedroom. "Lord, what a day! I'm glad to be home!" Michelle flopped down on the bed. She had let her staff go early for the holiday and thought she would be able to get a little more work done in the quietness. Not so. The phones kept ringing, the copier jammed and everything that could go wrong did.

Michelle turned over and looked at the clock. It was already six-thirty and she hadn't even figured out what to fix for dinner. She got up, changed clothes and went back to the kitchen. Her cell phone began chiming. "Hi, honey."

"Hey, baby. How are you?"

"Good. What about you?"

"I'm about the same. What are you doing?"

"I'm trying to decide what to cook for dinner. We need to be at church about nine o'clock if we want a decent seat."

"That's why I'm calling. I'm not going to make it back on time. I had an accident."

"What? Are you okay?" Michelle anxiously asked. "What happened? Where are you?"

"Slow down, baby. I'm okay," Michael reassured her. "I'm at a hotel."

"What happened?"

"The snow came earlier than predicted and started out as sleet. I was almost at the Mansfield exit when a car ahead of me hit a patch of black ice. He lost control and started a chain reaction. When it was all over, I ended up in a ditch, one of the other drivers has a broken leg and a couple of cars hit the guard rail. Fortunately, no one was seriously hurt, praise God."

"Yes, praise God. But why are you in a hotel?"

"The car rental places closed early so I can't get anything until tomorrow. I'm sorry, babe."

"I can come get you," Michelle offered.

"No. Absolutely not! I don't want you on the road."

"But..."

"No baby. I'm okay," Michael insisted. He didn't tell her that it was only by the grace of God his truck hadn't gone over the embankment. Landing in a ditch was no big deal compared to what might have happened.

"But, Michael, it's New Year's Eve!" They had planned a private celebration after church to commemorate their first New Year's together and she was looking forward to it. Now he was telling her it wasn't going to happen.

"I know, sugar, and I'm upset about it, too. But I won't take a chance on you driving in unpredictable weather. I'll be okay," Michael assured her. "I'm going to spend the night here and dream about you. As soon as its daylight, I'll find somebody to either repair the truck or I'll rent one; I'll even walk if I have to. Either way, I'll be home tomorrow." Michelle was too disappointed to respond. "Hey," he inquired softly, "Are you going to be okay?"

"Yeah. I just wish you were going to be here," Michelle mumbled. She didn't try to hide her disappointment.

"I know. Go on to church and call me when you get home, okay?"

"Okay."

"I'm sorry this happened. I love you."

"I love you, too."

A Hug From Daddy

Michael hung up the phone and sat quietly for a few moments. He removed the small Bible he always carried and turned to Psalm 145:

> I will extol you, my God, O King,
> And I will bless your name forever and ever.
> Everyday I will bless you.
> And I will praise your name forever and ever.
> Great is the Lord, and most worthy of praise;
> His greatness no one can fathom.

"Oh, Lord, I do praise you, and I love you."

I love you, too.

"I really wanted to be home tonight."

I know you did.

"Why couldn't I get there?"

I am going to do something special for Michelle and she needs to be alone tonight.

"Thank you, Father."

You are welcome, son.

"I want to be a good husband. Show me what I need to do, Lord."

You are doing everything you are supposed to do. The rest is up to her.

"But don't I need to be there for her?"

No. I have this one.

"So what am I supposed to do, Lord?"

The same thing you have been doing. Love, honor and cherish her as the precious gift she is. Protect her and pray for her.

"I do, Lord."

And continue to be there for her when she needs you.

"I will, Lord. I've always tried to show her how much she means to me from the very first day we met. I want to grow old with her by my side."

Do you trust me?

"You've brought me this far. How can I not trust you?"

Then trust me with Michelle. Everything is under control.

"Thank you, Father."

CHAPTER THREE

NEW YEAR'S DAY—EARLY MORNING

Michelle wasn't really surprised that Michael's truck wasn't in the garage. Throughout the church service she kept hoping he would have made it home and was disappointed when he didn't. She walked into the house, turned off the alarm, hung her coat in the hall closet and headed for their bedroom. There she kicked off her pumps and removed her suit jacket as she went to her side of the walk-in closet. Michelle was tempted to leave her clothes on the floor, but knew she couldn't give in to despair. She could feel depression trying to slip up on her and was determined to resist its pull.

Still in her slip, Michelle walked from the closet to the bathroom, removed her makeup and brushed her teeth. She sat on the side of the bed and checked the voice mail.

"Hi, babe. I know you're not there but I wanted to leave a message anyway. I'm sorry we can't be together tonight. I watched a New Year's Eve service on the television, but it wasn't the same. God has been good to us, and I wanted to thank Him while sitting beside the beautiful gift He's given me. It wasn't meant to be this year. God must be up to something; we just don't know what it is yet. I love you so very much. I just wanted you to hear my voice when you came in from church. So change your clothes, get a bowl of ice cream and call me. I'll be waiting."

Michelle played the message again. At least she could hear the soothing sound of his voice even if it wasn't in person. Michael was always the more optimistic one—"God must be up to something"—and she tried to embrace his optimism. But it hurt. They weren't together and she didn't like it. She saved the message and got up from the bed.

"Lord, thank you for my husband. I don't like what's going on, but it must be your will. Help me to accept it," Michelle prayed. She slipped into a hot pink silk nightshirt and went to the kitchen, fixed a bowl of peach ice cream, reset the alarm, turned off the lights and went back to the bedroom. She settled on the chaise with a throw around her legs and the ice cream on the table beside her. She then dialed her husband's cell phone.

"Happy New Year, baby," Michael crooned.

"Same to you," Michelle said.

"How was church?"

"It was great. You know Pastor preached!"

"I know he did!" Michael agreed. "How are you doing, sweetie?"

"I'm okay," Michelle replied softly.

"Just okay?"

"For now, just okay. I miss you. Your message helped, though."

"I miss you, too. But it's already a new year and I'll be home later today."

"I know."

"So tell me, how was church?" Michael asked again.

"It was good. There were a lot of people in attendance and Pastor preached on the topic "Set Up for a Comeback" out of John 11:1-4."

"And how many points did he have?" he asked. Pastor Jethro Hooper was well-known for having multiple points to his sermons although he insisted he only had three. It was just that those three points each had six points and sometimes the points even had points. Their pastor was a phenomenal preacher and teacher. His radio broadcasts were heard throughout most of the Midwest and it would just be a matter of time before he was seen on television.

Michelle chuckled, "You know he had a lot, but his main three were that God can raise dead things when we die to our plans, our past and people."

"Wow. Is that on target or what? Has he been listening to our conversations?" Michael asked. They were both self-employed and believed that the success of their businesses was directly due to the favor of God. They committed to keeping God first in their lives, marriage and business and didn't want anything to interfere with God's plans for them. Both had encountered the same obstacles—friends and family questioning the sanity of leaving highly paid positions with benefits and security to step out on their own—but God had shown Himself faithful by blessing their efforts.

"Yeah, it hit close to home for both of us. I bought a CD for you."

"Thanks babe. Anything else happen?"

"Something strange happened at the end of the service."

"Was it a good strange or a bad strange?"

"I don't know; it's hard to explain."

"Just give it a try."

"Well, earlier in the service, Pastor Hooper said that one of his daughters had come into his office praising God for having made it through this year. I guess it was a rough one. Then at midnight Pastor invited everyone to the altar for prayer. When I got back to my seat, I saw something that disturbed me, but I don't know why."

"What baby?"

"Well, when I got back to my seat, I looked up on the platform and saw Pastor hugging his daughter."

"The daughter that had made it through?" Michael clarified.

"Yes."

"Why would that bother you? It was just a hug, wasn't it?"

"Yes, but...Oh, I told you it was hard to explain."

"Take your time," Michael encouraged.

"I think what bothered me was that I realized I had never had a hug like the one they exchanged," Michelle confessed.

"What kind of hug was that?"

"I've never seen anything like it. It was like acceptance and love and protection and forgiveness all wrapped in one. It was such a powerful scene that I finally had to turn away before I started crying."

"I hug you all the time and I certainly accept, love, protect and forgive," Michael reminded her.

"I know honey, but you're not my father."

"Oh, so that's it."

"I think so. I think that's why it bothered me. My father never hugged me like that and now it's too late. I sometimes wonder how differently my life would have been if he had shown that kind of love and affection."

"I'm sorry baby. If I could take the hurt away, I would."

"I know."

"But you know what? God is your Father and He can hug you, too."

"I know," Michelle whispered.

"I know you do. The Bible reminds us that we can cast all our burdens on Him. Whenever you're ready, He can heal this hurt. I would if I could, but I'm not God. When you're ready to turn this over to Him, I'll be with you every step of the way. You know that, right?

"Yes."

"Okay baby. Did you eat your ice cream?"

"No," Michelle laughed. "It melted while I was talking to you."

"Sorry."

"It's okay. I probably didn't need it anyway. I'll never get rid of these twenty pounds eating ice cream every night."

"But those are my twenty pounds and I love them."

"You always know the right things to say."

"I do my best. Now, let's have a word of prayer and then I want you to get some sleep, okay?"

"Okay."

"Father, thank you for all you've done for us. You've been better than we deserve and we thank you. Lord, I'm asking you to do something special for us as we begin a new year. Take us to another level in you. Strengthen our marriage and bind the cords of our love tighter. Dispatch your angels to stand guard over us this night so that no hurt, harm or danger can come near. Keep my wife safe until I get home. We love you Lord and thank you for hearing our prayers. Amen."

"Amen."

"I'll see you later this morning. Love you."

"Love you back."

Michelle hung up the phone and marveled again at how blessed she was to have a husband who loved her and the Lord. She sat at her dressing table to braid her hair. The scene from church again flashed in her mind. There was something disturbing about it. Michelle told

Michael it was because she had never received a hug like that from her father, but she knew there was more to it than that. She finally gave voice to her inner thoughts. "Why did that bother me so much?"

You know why.

"Lord?"

Yes, child.

"Why couldn't I be loved like that?"

You are loved.

"I know my husband loves me... "

Yes he does. He is one of my favorite servants. His prayers will be answered.

"...And I believe you love me. But..."

I know child. When you are ready for the answer, I will be here.

"Oh, Lord, I can't deal with this now. It's going to hurt too much."

Michelle, Michelle. Pain always comes before healing.

"I don't think I can handle it."

Yes you can, Michelle. You are stronger than you think.

"I don't know about that."

But I do.

"You're right. I just don't think I can do this now."

Whenever you are ready.

Michelle went to bed, turned off the light and settled down under the covers. She stubbornly tossed and turned for almost two hours before finally sitting up. "Okay, God. Since I can't get any sleep, I might as well get this over with. Will you help me?"

Yes.

"So it's going to hurt?"

Some, but you will be okay. I will be with you.

"I'm going to hold you to that."

Just go to sleep. It will be all right.

Michelle snuggled back under the covers and wondered what was going to happen. She now knew why she felt that today was going to be life-changing. She was both excited and leery. She knew she had put off dealing with her issues long enough, but was she really ready to meet them head-on tonight? And how was God going to help her? What was He going to do? Michelle fell asleep pondering these questions.

God had already chosen to help Michelle by allowing her to re-member the specific events that shaped her attitude about Him, her parents and Michael. She might not have the most restful night, but it would be a productive one. He had put a powerful ministry inside her for hurting women and it was time for her to give birth to it. He had things He needed her to do, but she would first have to get past her own hurts.

CHAPTER FOUR

Most seven-year-old girls were bigger than Mimi, but that didn't stop her from trying new things. Today she was trying to master the art of double Dutch and had been at it most of the morning.

"Come on, Mimi, you can do it," Maria encouraged.

"Lift your feet up higher," Stephanie added.

"Okay," Mimi said, "I'll try." She took a deep breath and entered the ropes at just the right speed and just the right time. She jumped for a full two minutes before her feet got tangled in the ropes.

"I did it!" she shouted. "I'll be right back."

"Where are you going?" Maria asked.

"I'm going to tell Mommy. I'll be right back," she said again. Mimi ran through the back door and found her mother, Betty, snapping green beans with her sister-in-law, Shirley.

"Mommy! Guess what?"

"What baby?"

"I jumped double Dutch all by myself and didn't trip once."

"Good for you. I knew you could do it. You're a big girl, Sienna." Everyone else called her Michelle or Mimi, but her mother always called her by her first name. "Go tell your father what you did."

Mimi skipped into the living room and jumped on her father's lap. He angrily pushed her away. "What are you doing?"

"I w-wanted to tell you what I did o-outside," Mimi stammered.

"What is so important that you had to disturb me?" Donald Nickelson was irritated, again! At six feet, five inches and heavily built, he was an intimidating presence, especially since he very seldom smiled. "Don't you see me reading the paper?"

"Yes Daddy, but I w-wanted to tell you..."

"I don't care what you wanted to tell me. Stop bothering me. Either go back outside or go talk to your mother. I'm busy!"

Mimi's Uncle Carl had just come back from the store and heard the commotion. "Take it easy, Donald."

"Stay out of this Carl. This has nothing to do with you."

"B-But Daddy..." Michelle tried again.

"Don't 'but Daddy' me. Did you hear what I said?" Donald shouted.

"Y-Yes sir."

"Then get out of my sight!" He snapped the paper in place and went back to reading.

CHAPTER FIVE

22 YEARS AGO—SEPTEMBER 15

Michelle hadn't meant to eavesdrop on her parents. She was walking past their bedroom when she heard her name mentioned so she stopped to listen.

"Donald, why won't you spend more time with Sienna? She needs to have her father around."

"I am around," Donald snapped.

"But not for her."

"What do you want from me, Betty? I keep a roof over your head and food on the table. I give you money to go shopping. What more do you want?"

"I want you to spend time with your daughter," Betty insisted.

"I don't have time. That's why she has you."

"But she's growing up. Boys have already started to notice her..."

"She better not get pregnant," Donald interrupted.

Betty had been hearing this for the past two years and was sick of it. She didn't know what had caused this fixation with pregnancy. Every time she attempted to talk to Donald about it, they ended up having an argument. "It's not about her getting pregnant, Donald. It's about you spending time with your daughter. She's ten years old. The example you set today is what she'll expect from men in the future. It seems like you don't want to be bothered with her. Is that right?"

"No it's not right. You don't know everything, Betty," Donald fumed. "She has you."

"Donald, she needs us both," Betty pleaded.

"Well, I'm too busy!"

A Hug From Daddy

Michelle ran to her room, fell face down across the bed and vowed she wasn't going to cry. Tears didn't seem to do any good. Her father hated her and there was nothing she could do about it.

CHAPTER SIX

"I can't believe we have a test in algebra tomorrow," Stephanie moaned.

Mimi opened a pack of colored candies and popped two in her mouth before handing the bag to Stephanie. "Yeah, Miss Finch gives us too much homework anyway. Nobody else in the eighth grade gets as much as we do."

"Yeah," Stephanie agreed. She shook a handful of the candies out and handed the bag to Maria.

"Well, I guess it's for our own good," Maria responded logically as she handed the bag back to Mimi. "When I become a teacher, the kids will probably say the same thing about me." Maria had wanted to be a teacher since she was in the second grade.

"Whatever," Stephanie sniffed. "I don't see what rational and irrational numbers have to do with anything!"

"Me neither," Mimi agreed as she finished off the bag of candy. "Oh, well. I've got to get home. Mommy's fixing pork chops."

"Maybe I should go home with you," Maria offered.

"Come on," Michelle invited. "You know Mommy won't care."

"I can't. I've got to get home and watch Tiffany," Maria replied, referring to her younger sister. "But I sure love Miss Betty's pork chops."

"I guess that's more for me then," Michelle teased.

"Call me later," Stephanie hollered as she and Maria turned to go home.

"Okay." Michelle normally didn't mind walking home alone, but today she would have to pass that group of older boys standing on the corner. *I'll just walk past them really fast and maybe they'll let me alone,* she thought to herself. She began mentally going over coefficients, variables and other algebraic equations. Lost in thought Michelle didn't realize that one of the boys was following her.

CHAPTER SEVEN

Betty and Donald burst through the emergency room door and stopped at the information desk. "Someone called and said our daughter has been hurt. Her name is Sienna Michelle Nickelson. Where is she? How is she?" Betty anxiously asked. While the nurse was looking the name up, a doctor stopped at the desk. "May I help you?"

"We're here about our daughter, Sienna Michelle Nickelson," Betty repeated. "They said she was hurt and brought in a few minutes ago."

"I'm Dr. Glenn. I'm treating your daughter."

"What happened?" Betty asked.

"Let's step over here so we can talk." Dr. Glenn guided them to an enclosed area off the waiting room and encouraged them to sit down.

"What happened?" Betty demanded again. "I want to see my daughter."

"It's going to be a few minutes before I can take you back. She's going to need several stitches for a cut on her forehead."

"Is that all?" Donald sneered. "When the hospital called they acted like it was something more serious than a cut on the forehead. What's going on?"

"Mr. and Mrs. Nickelson, I'm afraid your daughter was attacked."

"Attacked?" Betty began rocking back and forth. "Who? Where?"

"Apparently she was on her way home from school when it happened. Two young men found her and brought her to the emergency room. One of them had brought a book bag that was beside her, which is how we found your number." Dr. Glenn glanced at the chart in his hand.

"Your daughter has been severely beaten. Her nose is broken, her arm is broken in three places and several teeth have been knocked out. She has a cut on her forehead that will require stitches and various bruises and scratches. All of that is expected to heal nicely." Dr. Glenn paused so they could digest what he had just said. Mrs. Nickelson was still rocking back and forth, but otherwise appeared to be doing okay. Mr. Nickelson stood rigidly in the corner with his arms folded.

"Your daughter was also raped and is going to require surgery to repair all the damage. The police are going to want to talk to you and your husband."

"Oh, my God! I need to see her." Betty stood up and looked around frantically. "Which way is she?"

"Just a minute Mrs. Nickelson. There's paperwork to fill out and you'll need to sign the consent form before we can begin treatment."

"I'll do it." Donald started toward the nurses' station.

"We will take precautions to prevent any sexually transmitted disease," Dr. Glenn continued.

"Is she pregnant?" Betty whispered.

"It's too early to tell, Mrs. Nickelson. We'll know in a few weeks."

"Where is Sienna? She must be going out of her mind."

"She's right back here. Try to compose yourself. Your daughter is already frightened," Dr Glenn cautioned. "After surgery she'll be moved to a regular hospital room. You're welcome to spend the night."

"Of course I'll spend the night," Betty assured him. "Donald and I both will."

CHAPTER EIGHT

Michelle was trying to work her way through a fog and could feel someone stroking her hand. "Wake up, sweetie. Your parents are here. Come on, wake up."

"What?" Where am I?" Michelle's mouth felt cottony and her entire body felt on fire, especially her face.

"Hi. Welcome back. My name is Penny and I'm your nurse." The voice belonged to a petite woman with blonde hair pulled back into a ponytail. "You're in the hospital. Let me get the doctor."

"No! Don't leave me," Michelle cried.

"It's okay honey. I'm just going right outside the door. You're safe here. Let me get the doctor." Penny gently pried Michelle's fingers from her arm. "I'll be right back."

Less than a minute later a tall gray-haired man walked in. On top of his head was a pair of black wire framed glasses and around his neck was a stethoscope. Michelle assumed this was the doctor. "Hello young lady. I'm Dr. Glenn," the man said confirming his identity. Sitting on the edge of the bed, Dr. Glenn took Michelle's hand and said, "How do you feel?"

"I hurt all over," Michelle mumbled. "Why is my arm in a cast? My nose feels funny, too."

"Your arm is broken. I expect it to mend correctly and you'll have no future problems. Your nose is broken and what you're feeling is the packing. You're also missing a few teeth. Your parents are outside, but let me just take a quick look at your eyes before they come in." Dr. Glenn pulled a small penlight from his jacket pocket and pointed it at Michelle's pupils. "Is that light too bright?"

"No, but my head hurts."

"That's to be expected. You have stitches in your forehead."

"Stitches?" Michelle started to touch her forehead and Dr. Glenn gently placed her hand back on the sheet. Michelle began screaming. "Mommy! Mommy!"

"She's right outside," Dr. Glenn assured her. "I'll go and get your parents."

Betty rushed into the room before Dr. Glenn could reach the door and sat on the spot he had just vacated. "Oh, baby. I was so worried about you. When the hospital called, I didn't know what to think."

"Mommy, what happened?" Michelle clumsily tried to hug her mother with her good arm.

Dr. Glenn nodded his head so Betty wrapped both arms around Michelle. "You were attacked on the way home from school."

"Attacked?"

"You were raped, baby. Some boy raped and beat you up."

Michelle began to cry uncontrollably. When the tears ended, Betty wiped Sienna's face with a tissue and kissed her cheek. "Honey, it's going to be all right. I don't know why this happened. I'm just glad you're okay."

"Where's Daddy?" Michelle whispered.

Betty moved aside so Sienna could see her father. "He's right here honey."

Michelle held out her good arm to her father. "Daddy..."

"What have you done this time?" Donald demanded.

"D-Daddy! What are you talking about?" Michelle shrunk down further in the bed.

"Donald," Betty scolded, "What's the matter with you?"

"Who's the boy?" Donald continued as if he hadn't heard Betty's question.

"T-The last thing I remember is me, Maria and Stephanie coming out of Smithy's..."

"I've told you about acting like a slut..."

"D-Daddy! How can you say that? I didn't do anything..."

"Shut up! I don't want to hear it," Donald shouted. "Every time I turn around, you're always doing something. Now this!"

"B-But I didn't do anything!" Michelle's strength was fading fast. Her father's response hurt, but she was too tired to care.

"I said shut up or so help me...." Donald took a threatening step toward Michelle, but Dr. Glenn stepped in between them.

"Mr. Nickelson, you're going to have to leave. I can't allow your daughter to be upset."

"Shut up!" Donald snarled. "This isn't your business."

"Donald, stop it!" Betty snapped. "What's the matter with you? Don't you see Sienna's in pain and all you're doing is hollering at her? She didn't do anything wrong."

"So she says."

"Shame on you! Do you think she asked to be raped and beaten?"

"I don't know, Betty. Look at her. It's no wonder some boy took her up on what she's advertising. She probably liked the attention."

"I've heard enough. Get out of this room," Betty demanded.

"Don't worry, I'm going. And find out if she's pregnant. I'm not taking care of any brats!"

Michelle sat straight up in bed and tried to catch her breath. Her heart was racing; her chest felt tight and sweat broke out on her upper lip. *Oh, God, I can't take this. Why am I remembering all of this stuff now?* Michelle went to the bathroom to get a drink and splash cool water on her face. "God," Michelle whispered, "I didn't know it was going to hurt this bad. I'm not sure I can do this."

Will you trust me to get you through the night?

"Yes."

Just remember you are not alone. You are safe, Michelle. Go back to sleep.

Michelle pulled the comforter off her bed and sat on the chaise lounge. *I'll just sit up all night,* she reasoned. *Maybe if I don't go back to sleep I can handle whatever else is coming.* She sat back and was asleep almost immediately.

CHAPTER NINE

12 YEARS AGO—MARCH 30

Michelle finished her shift at the record store and rode the escalator down to the street level to cash her paycheck. She usually deposited most of her check into her savings account, but today she was going shopping. The mall offered their employees discounts at all the stores, and Michelle planned to take full advantage of those discounts. After all, today was her birthday and that deserved a treat, didn't it?

A few hours later Michelle had accumulated quite a bit of stuff: a teal colored sweater, cream colored slacks, a pair of jeans, two pairs of shoes and a bracelet. And she still had money left. Exhausted, Michelle pulled her bags close and settled on the bench across from one of her favorite spots in the mall. The food court held a wide variety of choices from the golden arches to a three-star restaurant. She liked watching the people decide what to eat.

Michelle woke up early that morning thinking about her mother and had been doing so all day. Betty Nickelson always made Michelle's birthday special. She would cook her favorite meal—meatloaf, mashed potatoes, green beans and lemon meringue pie for dessert. Her mom would stick a candle in the middle of the meringue and sing happy birthday followed by a big kiss accompanied with smacking sounds. That ritual never failed to crack both of them up as they dissolved into laughter over the silliness.

Betty Nickelson died last year following complications from heart surgery.

Every time Michelle thought she was getting stronger something happened. Just like today. Her father forgot her birthday and acted like it was just another day. Mom would've remembered, Michelle reminded herself. She couldn't understand what she had done to make her father hate her, but she had decided a few years ago that she couldn't keep making it her problem. She was three months away from graduation. She didn't know how, but she was determined to get away from him, his drinking and the indifference. Since the rape, her father had made her life a living hell. She couldn't wait to leave.

Michelle wasn't going to spend any more time dwelling on her father's negativity. So what if he didn't remember her birthday. Maria and Stephanie had already called her this morning to wish her happy birthday, and they were going out for pizza later this evening. Plus, Michelle knew that her Aunt Shirley and Uncle Carl would stop by with their traditional birthday gift—underwear and socks. Aunt Shirley believed you couldn't have enough of either, and had been giving Michelle the same gift for as long as she could remember. Oh, well, happy birthday to me!

CHAPTER TEN

The house was too quiet and Michael Stephens knew he had to leave. He saw evidence of the love and care his mother, Mary, had put into making their house a home everywhere he turned. As he glanced around the room that had been his since he was old enough to sleep alone, he saw the growth marks on the wall that finally stopped when he reached his present height of six feet, three inches, and the football trophies she lovingly shined. Even the quilt on his bed had been hand-made by his mom.

Michael removed the funeral program from the top of his dresser and lovingly traced his mother's face. Oh, God, how am I going to make it without her? His mother was his everything—friend, encourager and sounding board. He and his father were close, but Michael and his mom had that special bond that only occurs between a mother and son. He had cried so much over the last few days that he didn't think he had any tears left. The funeral was yesterday.

If just one more person told him his mother was in a better place, Michael knew he was going to explode. He didn't know how his father and sister kept doing it—smiling, shaking hands and listening to the rhetoric. Yes, he knew she was in a better place. Yes, he knew she wasn't in pain anymore. Yes, he knew God would ease the hurt and fill the void. He knew all that, but this was his mom. He was being selfish and he didn't care. His mother was dead and it hurt. There would be no more phone calls or smiles. No more surprise care packages sent to his dorm. No more late night discussions sitting at the kitchen table. No more of anything.

Michael had to get out of the house! He picked up his jacket and baseball cap and left the bedroom. His sister, Brianna, was sprawled across her bed resting. He thought about asking her to go with him, but he really didn't want to be bothered with anyone today. He walked softly past her door so that he wouldn't disturb her.

He reached the family room and saw his father napping in the recliner with half of the newspaper on the floor where it had fallen off his chest. His father had to be exhausted. He had been coordinating relatives and friends over the past few days while making sure that he and Brianna were okay. Michael had taken both set of grandparents to the airport early this morning; the rest of the relatives still in town were either back at their hotels or at his cousins' houses. His parents had celebrated twenty-nine years of marriage almost six months ago and now his mother was gone. If Michael was hurting, Donavon Stephens was hurting more.

Michael sat at the kitchen counter to write a note. He stuck it on the bulletin board next to the phone and once again was bombarded with memories of his mother. Michael had made the board in seventh grade shop class. His mom made a big production of giving it a place of honor in the house and had finally decided to hang it in the kitchen since that was where they spent most of their time. All these years later, it was still being used as the family's point of communication. Everyone knew to check the bulletin board before asking any questions because anything of importance would be there.

Michael took his keys off the wall hook and headed for the front door. He had parked on the street because his mom's car was still in the garage. He turned the ignition on his Mustang and let it idle. He had no idea where he was going. His note said he was going to the mall, but he didn't have a real destination. He just needed to be alone for a while. His best friend had already gone back to school and he couldn't think of anyone else he wanted to be around. He drove aimlessly for almost an hour and was surprised to end up at the mall anyway. His father's birthday was next month so maybe instead of waiting until the last minute he'd pick up something today.

Michael rode the escalator down to his favorite bookstore. He noticed the girl as soon as the escalator reached the bottom. She looked about nineteen or twenty and was the prettiest girl he had seen in a long time. Whoa! What are you doing? Michael chastised himself. You just buried your mother yesterday. You didn't come to the mall looking for girls. The girl turned her head and Michael felt a jolt of recognition. He knew her from somewhere, yet he was sure they had never been formally introduced because he certainly would have remembered.

She was watching the people passing by and wasn't even aware of him approaching. "Hi. Can I sit here?"

She turned her head and glanced his way before shyly lowering her eyes. "I guess so." Michelle scooted to the far end of the bench and placed her packages between them.

He smiled and said, "My name is Michael. What's yours?"

She once again glanced briefly at him and mumbled, "Michelle," but didn't return his smile.

Michael blurted out the first thing that popped into his head. "Hey, M and M. Get it? Michael and Michelle."

For the third time Michelle glanced at Michael, only this time she didn't look away. "Yeah, I get it. But there is no M and M," and turned her body so he couldn't mistake the fact that she didn't want to be bothered.

He didn't know what to do. Michael knew he was good looking but he wasn't conceited. He was well built from his years of playing football, and girls had been telling him for as long as he could remember that they liked his smile and his dimples. Michael was very comfortable with the opposite sex, but something about this girl made him nervous. Who was she? Why was he feeling like he had been punched in the stomach? Michael was surprised to realize he had the jitters. All he needed was for his hands to start sweating and his voice to crack. Wouldn't that make a good impression? They sat in silence for a few minutes while he thought about what he could say or do to keep her sitting there. She had turned her body just enough to let him know that she wasn't interested in talking to him, but he needed to know who she was and what it was about her that was making him react like a school-boy. He was twenty years old, not twelve.

"So what did you buy?"

"What?"

"What did you buy?" Michael repeated, indicating the packages. "It looks like you did some serious shopping."

"I picked up a few things." Michelle couldn't figure out why he was still sitting there. She did everything but leave and he wasn't taking the hint! Since the rape she didn't spend a lot of time talking to boys, especially alone. He did seem nice, though, and he had a great sounding voice. And she wasn't immune to that smile, the dimples or those perfect white teeth either, but he probably already knew that.

"Don't I know you?"

Michelle was so surprised by such a lame line that she burst out laughing. "Is that the best you can come up with?"

Michael laughed, too. "No seriously. Didn't you go to Central High School?

"I still do. I'm a senior. Do you go there?"

"No, I graduated two years ago."

She finally looked directly at him. "Hey, I remember you now. You were on the football team, right?"

"Right, but I spent more time on the bench my senior year because of injuries."

"Yeah, I remember that now." Michelle felt better about talking to him since they had something in common. "So what have you been doing since high school?"

"I go to Ohio State."

"Did you get a football scholarship?"

Michael shook his head. "My football days are over. I was offered an academic scholarship and I work part time. I'm just home for a couple of weeks." Michael was glad Michelle had started to warm up to him. "What about you? Are you planning on going to college?"

"I'll go to Tri-C," Michelle said using the informal name for Cuyahoga Community College. "My grades are good, but not good enough for a full scholarship. With a partial scholarship and part time work, I'll be okay."

"If you stay focused, you can do it."

"That's my plan. The sooner I get my degree, the sooner I can leave here."

"Where will you go?

"Anywhere, as long as it's away from here."

"I hear you." The conversation lagged when the school topic ran its course.

"Well, it was nice talking to you." Michelle began gathering her bags.

Michael had to think of something quick or she was going to walk away. "Would you like to get some ice cream?" He knew he was reaching, but he didn't care.

"Ice cream?"

"Yeah, ice cream. You know that cold stuff that comes in a variety of flavors?" Michael teased. "Don't you eat ice cream?"

"I love ice cream. Matter of fact, I have a bowl every night right before I go to bed," Michelle admitted.

"You're kidding."

"No, I'm serious. Since I was little my mother and I would have a bowl of ice cream every night."

"Then maybe we can go get a burger. I don't want to interfere with you and your mom's ritual."

"That's okay," Michelle sadly replied. "My mom died last year."

"Oh, Michelle. I'm sorry. That must have been rough."

"Yeah, it still is."

"I would think so."

Michelle made a quick decision. "Yes. I would like some ice cream." Maybe it wouldn't hurt to have ice cream with Michael. After all, they were in a public place and it was her birthday. She was planning to have ice cream anyway, so why not have it with him? Besides there was something that just felt safe about Michael, and she actually felt more curious than scared.

"Let's go. Then I'll drive you home."

"No." Michelle stopped gathering her bags and turned to look at Michael.

"No you don't want any ice cream or no I can't drive you home?"

"Yes to the ice cream, no to the ride."

"How did you get here? Did you drive, walk or take the bus?"

"I walked," Michelle said.

"Okay. Can I walk you home?"

"What about your car?"

"I'll leave it here, walk you home and then come back and get it."

"That's crazy." Michelle started laughing at the absurdity of the offer.

"Yeah, I know." Michael laughed, too. "But that's okay. Is it a deal?"

"Sure."

"What's your favorite flavor?"

"I love butter pecan and strawberry and peach and..."

"Whoa. I guess I should have asked what don't you like."

"Hmm, let's see. I don't care for black walnut. Other than that, I guess I like it all. What about you?"

"I love banana splits with extra cherries." Michael led her to the table and then went to place their order. They sat in companionable silence while eating their treats. Michael finished first and he asked Michelle if he could see her while he was in town.

"I guess so," Michelle shyly responded.

"If you give me your phone number, I'll call you to set something up while I'm here. When I get back to school, I'll have to concentrate to make up for the time I've been gone."

"That's fine with me. I don't date a lot," Michelle confessed.

"Why not? You're very pretty. I love your eyes. And your hair."

"Thank you."

"So why don't you have a bunch of guys following you around?"

"I don't want that."

"Why not?" Michael persisted.

"I just don't," Michelle snapped and then took a deep breath. "Can we talk about something else?" she asked more calmly.

"Sure. What do you want to talk about?"

"Why did you come home in the middle of the semester?"

"My mother died."

"Oh, my goodness, Michael. I am so sorry! When? How? I mean..."

"It's okay. She died last week and the funeral was yesterday. I needed to get out of the house and ended up at the mall."

"How are you handling things?"

"I'm not. But I turned it over to the Lord and asked Him to help me get through this. My mother and I were real close. She had been sick for awhile and the doctor said she wouldn't last much longer. It's funny, though. Even when you know someone is near death, it's still a shock when it actually happens."

"I know. My mother was my best friend and I just feel abandoned."

"I know the feeling. What about your father?"

"He's around. We're not close, though," Michelle admitted.

"That's too bad. Dad and I are close. It was just me, my sister and our parents. We're a tight knit family."

"How's your family handling things?"

"We're all getting through. God is going to help us," Michael said.

"God?" Michelle asked skeptically.

"Do you believe in God?"

"Sure, doesn't everybody?"

"Surprisingly, no. Do you go to church?"

"I went a few times with my mother, but my father thinks it's all a waste of time."

"How old are you?"

"I turned eighteen today," Michelle boasted. "That's why I went shopping."

"You're kidding. Happy birthday, Michelle!" Michael dramatically cleared his throat and then gave a very passable rendition of the birthday song.

Michelle clapped softly. "Thank you. I've never had a stranger sing happy birthday to me before."

"I'm not a stranger. We've shared ice cream together so that makes us at least acquaintances, right?"

"Right."

Michael cleared their table and asked Michelle if she was ready to go and she agreed. On the walk to Michelle's house, Michael picked up his earlier conversation. "You're an adult now so you don't need your father to take you to church. You can go on your own."

"Maybe."

"You can come to church with me while I'm home and maybe you'll decide it's something you want to keep doing," Michael offered. "I think you would like our church. We have a great youth pastor and a lot of young adults. You would fit right in."

"Okay, I'll think about it."

About twenty minutes later they arrived at Michelle's house. "I liked being with you today," Michael said as he handed her back the bags. "Did you have a good time?"

Michelle smiled and nodded her head. "Thanks for making my birthday special."

Michael bent down to kiss her cheek. "You are very welcome, Michelle. I'll call you tomorrow, okay?"

CHAPTER ELEVEN

The car had scarcely stopped before Michael bounded from it and took the steps three at a time. "Hey, Dad, where are you?" Michael hollered as he came through the front door.

"I'm in the kitchen." His father had just finished making a roast beef sandwich on wheat bread with lettuce, tomatoes, red onions and mayo. He automatically started making another sandwich when he heard Michael at the door. "Where've you been? Your note said you were going to the mall and coming right back."

Michael slid into the kitchen chair before responding. "Dad, how did you know Mom was the woman you were going to marry?"

"What brought that on?" his father asked as he finished preparing the second sandwich.

"Well, I went to the mall like I told you. When I got there I saw this girl and it was like I had been hit in the chest. We talked, had some ice cream and I walked her home."

"Walked her home? What's wrong with your car?"

"There's nothing wrong with it. I walked Michelle home and then went back to the mall to get the car."

"Her name's Michelle?"

"Yes sir. Michelle Nickelson."

"So let me understand this," Donavon said as he held a pitcher of lemonade in his hand. "You drove to the mall, met some girl, invited her for ice cream, walked her home, walked back to the mall and then drove back home. Right?"

"Right."

"And the first question you ask me is how did I know your mother was the woman for me?"

"Yes sir. I know it sounds crazy, but I believe I just met my wife."

"Well I'll be," Donavon said as he took a seat. "That's great! And just for the record, you're not crazy."

"I'm not?" Michael took a large bite of his sandwich and nodded his appreciation to his father.

"No, you're not. I saw your mother at a church picnic when I was visiting my cousin in Arkansas. She was seventeen and the prettiest girl I had ever seen. I introduced myself to her and offered to get her some punch. She turned me down. I asked if I could push her on the swing and she turned me down again. I asked her if I could walk her home and she turned me down for that, too. But I was determined that I was going to get to know her. She was so pretty and I felt an instant connection to her although she was ignoring me." Donavon smiled as he remembered that time so long ago.

"Anyway, I was in Arkansas for the summer so every chance I had I would try to talk to her. She finally had pity on me and let me buy her an ice cream soda at the drugstore. Once she started talking to me she realized I wasn't such a bad guy and one thing led to another. But I knew the first time I saw her that she was going to be in my life. I just didn't know it was going to take time to convince her of the same thing."

Donavon used the back of his hand to wipe his eyes before continuing. "Wow. I haven't thought of that in a long time."

"I'm sorry Dad. I didn't mean to make you sad." Michael's own eyes were a little damp.

"It's okay, son. I'm sad because she's gone, but I don't regret one moment of the time Mary and I spent together. Your mother was my best friend and my companion. I pray that you and your sister will find the same kind of love."

"I think I did today."

"So did you get her phone number?" Donavon pulled himself together and took a bite of his forgotten sandwich.

"Sure did. I told her I would call her tomorrow. I invited her to church."

"That's good. Is she a Christian?"

"I don't think so."

"Well, just be careful, son."

Michael stuffed the last of his sandwich in his mouth. "I will Dad. I think I'll go call her now."

"I thought you were going to call her tomorrow?" Donavon chuckled.

"I can't wait to talk to her again."

"Okay. I'll go in the other room so you can have some privacy."

"Thanks, Dad. And thanks for the sandwich, too." Michael dialed the number Michelle gave him. A rough sounding man answered. "Yeah, who's calling me?"

"Hello, may I speak to Michelle please."

"Who's this?"

"Is this Mr. Nickelson?"

"Yeah."

"I'm a friend of your daughter's."

"How you know my girl?"

"I met her at the mall today."

"Today? And you just couldn't wait to talk to her again, I suppose. How old are you boy?" Donald belligerently asked.

"I'm twenty."

"Well, you're too old to be sniffing around my girl. She's only seventeen."

"I don't mean to be rude, sir, but she's actually eighteen. Today's her birthday."

"Don't tell me about my own kid. I know how old she is!"

"Yes sir. Can I speak to Michelle?" Michael persisted.

"Listen, I don't know what your game is. But my girl don't need some slick talker sniffing around her like a dog in heat. Don't call my house again!"

"But sir..."

"You heard me," he shouted. "Now get off my phone!"

Michael was still holding the phone in his hand when Donavon walked back into the kitchen with his dirty dishes.

"Did you talk to her?"

"Not exactly."

"Wasn't she home?"

"I don't know. Her father answered the phone. I think he was drunk and he wouldn't let me talk to her. He said he didn't need some slick talker sniffing around his daughter like a dog in heat and then slammed the phone down."

"That's too bad, son."

"He didn't even know that today was her birthday."

"Listen, Michael. I know you're hurting for your new friend, but you can't go against her father's wishes. If he doesn't want you calling his house, then don't," Donavon cautioned.

"But how is she supposed to be my wife if I can't talk to her?"

"You're going to have to trust God to work it out. If it's meant for you to be together, then no matter what happens, you'll be together. You just have to trust that God knows more about this situation than you do."

CHAPTER TWELVE

6 YEARS AGO—DECEMBER 21
COLUMBUS, OHIO

Michelle marked her place in the book she was reading and picked up her ringing cell phone. "Hello."

"Hey, girl. What's up?"

"Nothing much, Nikki." Michelle had met Nicole Peterson at the gym almost three years ago and they had become good friends. They often laughed at how much they had in common: They had both moved to Columbus about the same time with Michelle coming from Cleveland and Nikki coming from New Mexico. They lived in the same area of town one street apart and had actually closed on their condos within two weeks of each other. They both held MBAs from the same school although they graduated three years apart; and they liked going to the clubs. That's where the similarities ended. Michelle was five foot eight and voluptuous, Nikki was five foot three, dainty and cute. She had hair the color of mahogany that she wore in a classic bob. Her skin was lightly tanned and she had hazel eyes that were more green than brown; a gift from her European mother and black father.

"Girl, didn't we have fun last night?" Nikki gushed.

"Sure," Michelle half-heartedly responded. They had gone to a new club geared toward professionals. It was a nice place, but Michelle spent most of the night bored.

"Did you notice that fine brother that was hitting on Janet?"

"How could I miss him? He was the best looking thing in the place," Michelle admitted. "Did they leave together?"

Nikki snickered. "Knowing her they did." Michelle could hear Nikki lighting a cigarette and taking that first puff. "And who warmed your sheets last night?"

"Nobody," Michelle responded. "I just didn't feel like being bothered. I'm getting tired of doing the same old thing. You know, go to the club, have some drinks, let some man hit on you and go home to either his place or yours. I think I'm getting too old for this stuff."

"Yeah, right grandma," Nikki laughed. "What are you all of twenty-five?"

"Twenty-six! But I have been doing this since I was nineteen." Michelle tried to find the words to express her frustration. "Don't you ever get tired of doing the same thing? Don't you wonder if there's something more or if this is all there is?"

"No, girl, I don't. Right now I like what I'm doing," Nikki responded. "So I guess you're not going to the club tonight?"

"No. I think I'm going to stay home and chill."

"Okay then. I'll talk to you later."

Michelle hung up the phone, went to the kitchen and poured a glass of wine. She took the wine with her to the bedroom and removed her stash of reefer from the nightstand. Her phone rang just as she was getting ready to light up. A smile lit her face when she recognized the number.

"Hey, sweet thing. What's shakin'?"

"Hey, baby." Michelle knew her evening just got better. She had met Amari Benson almost a year ago at a mixer she and Nikki had attended. They started dating almost immediately, although not exclusively. "I'm just taking life easy."

"How about doing that over here? I sure could use some of your sweet stuff."

"I don't know. I was planning on staying in all night."

"Fine. I'll come to you," Amari suggested. "You know I'll make it worth your while, Mimi. Don't I know exactly how to relax you? Besides it's been a while since we hooked up. I miss you."

"I miss you, too," Michelle acknowledged.

"Then let me come over."

"Okay. Give me about an hour." Michelle hung up the phone and laughed. So much for not doing the same old thing, she thought. She started running bath water and sipped her wine while waiting for the tub to fill. She decided that she would wear white silk lounging pajamas with a camisole. She knew she wouldn't be wearing them long.

CHAPTER THIRTEEN

Michelle never remembered how bad a hangover felt until she had one. Between the wine and the reefer she had a splitting headache. She eased into a sitting position and gingerly held her head. *Why do I keep doing the same stupid things over and over?* Michelle chastised herself. Something had to change. She looked at a sleeping Amari and decided to begin with him. Michelle roughly pushed his shoulder to get his attention. "Amari. Wake up!"

"Hey, sweet thing," he drawled and glanced at the clock. "Why did you wake me up so early?" It was ten-fifteen in the morning, but since they didn't go to sleep until the sun came up, Michelle imagined he would think that was early. "Didn't I give you enough last night?" Amari stroked Michelle's leg.

Michelle slid from the bed and reached for her robe. "You need to leave."

"Say what?" Amari sat up in the bed causing the sheet to slip to just below his navel.

"I want you to get dressed and leave. Now."

"What's the matter with you? Why you trippin'?" Amari scratched his stomach. "Come back to bed."

"I'm not trippin'. I want you to get up, get dressed and get out of my house."

"I don't know what your problem is. You weren't so eager for me to leave last night. Matter of fact, you were tearing my clothes off as soon as I walked in the door."

"That was last night. This is a new day."

"Okay. Okay. I'm leaving." Amari sat on the side of the bed. "Can I at least take a shower first?"

"No. You can shower at your own house."

"Oh, so it's like that, huh?" Amari demanded while standing up. He turned to face Michelle in his nakedness as if daring her to turn down his silent offer. "Are you sure about that?"

"Yeah, I'm sure." Michelle went to the bathroom and closed the door. A few minutes later she heard the front door slam and knew she was alone. Michelle returned to her bedroom and sat on the side of the bed. What is the matter with me? Michelle thought. She knew she had all the trappings of success—the right car, the right address, the right career, plenty of friends. She had a variety of lovers to accommodate any of her moods. She was blessed with good looks and a nice figure so why wasn't she happy?

Michelle suddenly thought about David Watters, a man who worked in her building. He was tall, dark and handsome, but every time she flirted with him he acted like he didn't know what was going on. It had to be that church stuff he was always talking about. She heard he taught a Bible study in their office building and every time she saw him he managed to insert something about Jesus into the conversation. If he wasn't so fine, she'd stop talking to him all together. One of these days she would wear him down, Michelle vowed to herself. But this morning she wasn't thinking about how to get him in bed. She was remembering a conversation they had earlier in the week.

"David, some of us are going to the club after work. Do you want to join us?" Michelle always extended the invitation knowing he was going to turn her down.

"No thanks, Mimi," David replied, true to form.

"Why not? Are you too good for us?" She asked. Michelle knew the only reason she antagonized David was because he wasn't paying any attention to her.

"It's not that. I have something else to do."

"Well then maybe I'll go with you," Michelle mischievously responded.

"You're more than welcome," David invited. "I'm going to a Bible study at my church. We would love for you to join us."

"No thanks. I'm not into that holy roller stuff."

"No just the club stuff, right?" David stooped down to look Michelle in the eye. "Does that make you happy?"

"What would you know about the club?" Michelle asked indignantly. "You just look like a church boy. Am I right? You've probably never tasted a drop of liquor, smoked a joint or heaven forbid fooled around with a woman."

"You don't know anything about me," David replied softly.

"I know that all of you Christians are alike," Michelle retorted. "You love to look down on people who aren't like you so you can feel superior. I don't need that."

"I don't know who's been talking to you, but real Christians don't look down their nose at anyone. The Bible says that all have sinned, including me. But God gave me a chance to put my life back together so that the things I used to do, I don't do anymore. He will do the same for you."

"No thanks. I like my life just the way it is."

"Okay, Mimi." David began walking away. "When you change your mind, we're the Christian Center located on Thompson Lane. You can't miss us. Come by any Sunday. Service starts at ten-forty-five. Like I said, we would love to have you join us."

Michelle wondered why she was thinking about that conversation now. David certainly didn't act like any of the other men she knew. The harder she tried to get in his pants, the harder he tried to get her in church. Maybe there was something to this Jesus stuff after all. She glanced at the clock and saw that it was ten-fifty. David said service started at ten-forty-five and she was already late. Oh, well, maybe I'll go next Sunday, she reasoned.

Michelle swallowed two aspirins to take the edge off her headache and headed for the shower. She took her time and let the water ease the aches and pains of a long night. Michelle felt a lot better when she turned the water off fifteen minutes later. Making a quick decision, Michelle was determined that late or not, headache or no headache, she was going to church.

Looking through her closet trying to find a suitable outfit, Michelle finally decided on a black pantsuit. She didn't know if they wore pants in David's church but it didn't matter. It was either pants or one of her short skirts and she didn't think God would appreciate her coming in dressed for the club. Michelle grabbed her purse, slipped on her shoes and headed for the garage.

CHAPTER FOURTEEN

Michelle eased her BMW into a parking spot and walked quickly to the church. Standing in the vestibule she could hear the preacher. She quietly opened the door and the usher motioned her in with a smile and handed her a bulletin. She indicated that Michelle should sit on the second row from the back, which was fine with her. She certainly wasn't interested in walking all the way to the front. She didn't have a lot of experience with church, but she believed it was one thing to be fashion-ably late to a party; it was something else to come late for church and then go all the way to the front to find a seat. The second row from the back was fine.

Michelle scanned the bulletin and paused when she saw the sermon topic: "It's Never Too Late to Start Over." She wondered if this was some kind of sign from God. The preacher was saying, "There's someone here today that believes they can never start over again. They think they've made such a mess of their life that nothing can be done about it. Well, you're wrong. God is the God of another chance. Not just a second chance, but another chance." Michelle remembered David saying almost the same thing.

"And I guarantee that if you take one step toward Him," the preacher continued, "He will bring you in the rest of the way. There's nothing you've done that is so bad that the blood of Jesus can't cleanse you, and the forgiving power of God can't reach you. If you're tired of the direction your life has taken; if all the so-called trappings of success still leave you unfulfilled, if you've come to the end of your rope and don't know what to do, try Jesus. He will be the greatest thing that will ever happen to you. Trust Him with your life."

Michelle wondered how the preacher knew what she had been thinking. It was almost as if he could read her mind. She wouldn't have been surprised if he called her by name and said, "Yes, Michelle, I'm talking to you." She knew she wasn't happy, but was she ready to change her life this drastically? Was it really that easy? Michelle thought of how crazy her lifestyle was and knew that no matter what, she couldn't continue the path she was on. At this rate, she would be dead before her thirtieth birthday.

While the domination for her soul was going on, the preacher kept extending the invitation to accept Jesus. "The Bible says that when you're in Christ, you're a new creation. The old has passed away and the new has come. That means it's never too late to start over. Come on to Jesus. Step out in faith and come to this altar and turn your life around. It will be the greatest decision you'll ever make. My brothers and sisters, you don't have to leave here the same way you came in. Come on to Jesus now."

Somehow Michelle found herself at the altar, crying and surrendering her life to Jesus. An older woman hugged her and led her in prayer. When she whispered amen, she felt lighter, almost as if she could float away. Michelle was sent to a small room to fill out paperwork where she discovered that the woman who prayed with her was Sister Viola Henderson. The new members were encouraged to stay for a welcome reception where they would meet the pastor, his wife, their prayer partner and some of the leaders of the church.

"Welcome to the family of God," a young woman said as she walked toward Michelle with a smile on her face. She was close to six feet tall and slender. She was an attractive woman with a short curly hairstyle and wireless glasses.

"Thank you," Michelle smiled in return.

"My name is Sarah Caldwell and I'll be your prayer partner."

"Michelle Nickelson. It's nice to meet you," Michelle said as they shook hands. "What does a prayer partner do?"

"My responsibility is to pray for you. I'll also be available if you just want to talk or if you have questions and things like that. The next twenty-four hours are going to be pretty rough." Sarah handed her a business card which read, Sarah Caldwell, Ph.D. "This has all of my numbers on it, so you can call me anytime day or night."

"What's so special about the next twenty-four hours?" Michelle inquired.

"The devil is going to be busy. He'll try to plant thoughts and ideas in your head telling you that you've made a mistake, you'll never be able to change and things like that. People from your former life will probably either call or stop by. You aren't strong enough to withstand this assault by yourself so that's why we assign prayer partners to new members."

"You're right. I don't know anything about the church or assaults from the devil or any of that stuff," Michelle confessed. "I just know that what used to make me happy wasn't doing it anymore. Or maybe I was never happy. I was talking with someone who attends here the other day and he asked me if I was happy. That started me thinking about just how unfulfilled my life really is. I make good money, have a nice car, bought a house in a good neighborhood, but it just doesn't seem to be enough. Something was missing, you know?"

"Yes I do." Sarah acknowledged. "The missing link is Jesus Christ. But you accepted Him today and your life will never be the same."

"Is that true?"

Sarah nodded her head. "We may not have the same experiences, but every Christian has a turning point in their life when they realize there's a giant hole in their soul that can only be filled with Jesus Christ. That's why I said welcome to the family of God. It's bigger than a church or a denomination. It's universal!"

"Wow. I'm going to need all the family I can get."

"We'll be here for you," Sarah assured her. "Let's get some refreshments and we'll talk more."

"Okay. I trust you to lead the way."

"No, we're both trusting God to direct our steps. That's the only way to make it." They filled their plates with finger sandwiches and cookies before the conversation resumed. "So you know one of the members here?" Sarah asked.

"Yes. David Watters. Do you know him?"

"Sure. Everybody knows David. Do you work with him?"

"We work in the same building and he invited me to church. Actually he's invited me several times and this morning I decided to accept his offer." Michelle became overwhelmed by all that had happened in such a short time. "I'm so glad I did," she tearfully whispered.

Sarah hugged Michelle and suggested they find David so she could say hello. A few minutes later they approached him as he was finishing a conversation with another new member. Sarah tapped him on the shoulder to get his attention, "Look who's here."

"I see," David smiled. "Hey, Mimi."

"Hi, David."

"Welcome to the family of God."

"Thank you."

"I was glad to see you go to the altar. I'm proud of you, girl." David gave Michelle a brief hug. "More importantly, God is smiling."

"God doesn't smile." Michelle had never heard of such.

"Sure He does," David insisted. "God smiles whenever one of His children comes back home. The Bible says that the angels in heaven throw a party when someone gets saved."

"Really?"

"Yeah, it's party time in heaven," David said while dancing around.

"Wow!"

"Yeah, wow! So Sarah's your prayer partner. You'll get along great."

"She seems very nice," Michelle agreed.

"She is," David smiled in Sarah's direction and briefly squeezed her shoulder. "This is my favorite person here. I'm glad she got assigned to you. You're in good hands."

"Stop, you're making me blush," Sarah said laughing. Her bronze complexion had taken on a rosy glow.

"I know Sarah explained about the next twenty-four hours."

"Yes."

"I'll be praying for you, too. A lot of the saints here will be praying for you and the other new members throughout this week. And you know we have noon Bible study at the office on Tuesday and Thursday, so feel free to join us whenever you can."

"Thanks David. I appreciate both you and Sarah."

"It's our pleasure to get you rooted and grounded in the things of God. One day you'll do the same for someone else. It's a never-ending circle."

CHAPTER FIFTEEN

Michelle drove home in amazement; who would have thought so much could happen in such a short period of time. She went to church a sinner and was coming home a saint! She hadn't realized how much she was being weighed down until the weight was lifted. Her cell phone vibrated just as she pulled into her garage. "Hello."

"Hey, sweet thing, it's me. How ya doing?"

"I'm fine, Amari." Darn! That would teach her not to check her caller ID.

"Are you still mad at me?"

"I wasn't mad at you," Michelle truthfully responded. She was disgusted with herself, not him.

"Could have fooled me," Amari retorted. "Ooo wee, girl. You wore me out last night. I'm still feeling the effects of your good loving. How about I come over for a repeat performance since you ain't mad no more?"

"I don't think so. I'm not into that stuff anymore." Michelle's headache was coming back with a vengeance. Funny, she had all but forgotten about it until now.

"Since when? Because last night you couldn't get enough," Amari quickly reminded her.

"Last night I was a sinner. This morning I gave my life to the Lord. And I'm not into that stuff anymore," Michelle explained as best she could.

"Yeah, right! You're telling me that just that quick you lost interest in sex? What kind of mess is that?" Amari laughed.

"It's not mess." Michelle was determined to stand her ground. "And yes, I'm telling you that I'm changing my life. The Bible says that once I accept Jesus Christ as my Savior, I become a new person. The old person is dead and gone."

"Oh, so now you're quoting the Bible?" Amari scoffed. "Since when? Next thing you'll be telling me I need to change my life, too."

"Well you do, but that's up to you. All I know is that I wasn't happy with the way my life was going. I went to church, accepted Jesus Christ and feel better than I've ever felt in my life."

"Whatever." Amari dismissed what she was saying. "Listen, call me when you stop trippin'."

Michelle slapped the phone shut and it immediately started ringing. She checked the caller identification this time and saw that it was Nikki.

"Hey, Mimi, whatcha doing?"

"I just came home from church," Michelle replied as she walked into the kitchen.

"Say what?"

"Yeah, girl," Michelle laughed. "I went to church and got saved."

"From what?"

"Not what...well, I guess it was what..."

"What?"

"Remember when I asked you if there wasn't something more than what we were doing, you know, clubbing and whatever?"

"Yeah, so?"

"I found what was missing from my life."

"Mimi, you're not making sense."

"Okay, let me start over." Michelle paused to rub the back of her neck. "When I hung up from talking with you last night I really was planning on staying home alone. I was going to smoke a little weed, sip a little wine, and listen to jazz and chill. Then Amari called."

"Oh, boy," Nikki said. "I know where that led."

"Exactly. He came over and spent the night. But this morning when I woke up I didn't feel good about what I had done. I started thinking about a conversation I had with David..."

"Who?"

"David. Remember the man I told you about from work?"

"Yeah, I remember. You said he was always talking about Jesus."

"Right. Our last conversation was Thursday and he asked me if I was happy doing what I was doing. That got me to thinking and I decided that I wasn't happy. The things I thought would make me happy only lasted for a little while. I needed something more, but I didn't know what the something more was. This morning when I woke up with another headache from another hangover I knew I had to change the way I was living. I decided to go to church just to see what David was talking about and I ended up giving my life to Jesus."

"Wow, girl. That's deep."

"Yeah, it is. I still can't believe what happened."

"So do you feel any different?" Nikki asked.

"Actually I do, but it's hard to explain. I guess the best way would be to compare it to a huge weight being lifted off my shoulders. I feel free."

"Hmm."

"I know. It sounds strange, but it's true. I've never felt anything like this before in my life and I hope this feeling never goes away."

"So does this mean you won't be hanging out with a sinner like me?"

"We can still do some things together, you know movies and dinner and stuff. But I'm not going to the club and I'm not getting high."

"What about Amari?"

"And no more Amari!"

"Well, girl, if you feel this is what you need to do then I'm happy for you. Just don't try to convert me. I had my fill of Jesus growing up."

"Don't worry. I don't even know what I'm doing, let alone try to convert somebody else." Michelle thoughtfully closed the phone. Had she made a mistake? Was she going to lose all of her friends? Was she ever going to have fun again? Even before the thought had finished, Michelle remembered the so-called fun she had been having—hangovers, one night stands and false friends. Why not give Jesus a chance? It certainly can't be any worse than it already is. Michelle also remembered what Sarah and David had said about the first twenty-four hours and realized that the devil didn't waste any time getting busy. She'd have to really be on guard.

If Amari and Nikki couldn't get with the new Michelle, there were a few people in her life who would be thrilled that she was no longer operating under the control of the devil. Michelle hummed to herself as she dialed a familiar number. Maria, Stephanie and Michelle had been friends since they were five years old. Over the years, they always managed to keep in touch, no matter what was going on in each other's lives. Even though Maria and Steffie were both saved, Michelle knew that they loved and accepted her the way she was. Steffie had e-mailed Mimi a few days ago and closed with her customary line, "I'm praying for you." Michelle couldn't wait to tell her friend that the prayer had been answered today.

That night, Michelle knelt at her bed and prayed for the first time in her life. She didn't know the right words and just talked from her heart. She didn't have a Bible so she couldn't find the scripture the pastor had talked about, but she remembered what he had said. The old way was gone. Michelle told Jesus that was what she wanted Him to do for her: give her a new life. She finished praying and slept better than she had in a long time.

CHAPTER SIXTEEN

THIS YEAR —MAY 20
COLUMBUS, OHIO

"Stop, Sarah," Michelle panted. "I can't go any further."

Sarah immediately slowed her pace and looked at her friend with concern. "Can you make it to the water fountain?"

"Sure," Michelle gasped indignantly. "I'm just winded, not dying." Sarah and Michelle started out as prayer partners and the relationship evolved into friendship. They recently started walking in the park Monday through Friday as part of their new exercise routine. They tried to add a half mile every other week and were now up to eight miles a day, but the first few days of the additional half mile were always tougher on Michelle than Sarah.

"What are you doing the rest of the day?" Sarah waited for Michelle to finish drinking.

"Washing my hair, getting ready for next week," Michelle stepped aside for Sarah to get a drink. "You know, the usual."

"Girl, we're pitiful!" Sarah exclaimed. "Here we are two fine, intelligent women without a date on a Friday night."

"I hear you," Michelle responded and then started laughing. "You know we don't have to be dateless. It's a choice we've made."

"Yeah, I know. Didn't you go out with Brandon a few days ago?"

"Yeah."

"And...?" Sarah asked hopefully.

"Nothing! No spark. No chemistry. No nothing. He spent the whole evening going on about his ex-wife."

"I didn't know he was divorced."

"For four years, girl, and still stuck! I couldn't wait to get home."

"I can imagine."

"What about you?" Michelle asked.

"What about me?"

"Don't try to act all innocent with me Sarah Denise Caldwell. You have someone you could go out with every night if you wanted to."

"I have no idea what you're talking about."

"Don't even try it! You know that David would take you out in a heartbeat."

"No he wouldn't."

"Yes he would! What's the matter with you? That man is fine, you hear me? F-I-N-E! And he has all the qualities you say you want in a man. So what's the problem?"

"There is no problem," Sarah mumbled.

"I know you like David."

"As a friend."

"So tell me the truth. Is that's all he can ever be?"

"I don't know," Sarah mumbled again.

"Sarah, what's going on with you two?"

"I'm not sure."

"Can you talk about it?"

"I don't want to burden you, girl. You listen to my problems all the time."

"So what else are friends for? And it's not like you haven't helped me. Let me help you, if I can."

"Okay, maybe it would help to say it out loud. Let's sit down." They found a bench under a shade tree and sat down. "I know this is going to sound crazy, so I'll just say it." Sarah untied her shoe and rubbed her foot. "Just for the record, I like David. A lot. As a matter of fact, I know he's someone I could easily fall in love with…"

"I knew it!" Michelle interrupted. "I knew there was something going on with you two…"

"Mimi…"

"This is great! You two make such a cute couple, both tall, both …

"Mimi…"

"…smart. And I know David feels the same way about you. I've seen the way he looks at you and you just ignore the poor man…"

"Mimi!" Sarah shouted.

"What?"

"It's not going to happen."

"Sure it is. You just said you could fall in love with the man."

"It's not going to happen. We won't be getting together."

"Why not Sarah? What could possibly keep you two from beginning a relationship?"

"I can't get involved with him or any other man."

"That doesn't make sense."

"It doesn't have to make sense to you or anyone else. It's just the way things are."

"But why?" Michelle persisted.

"Because I can't leave my mother alone."

"*What?* You and your mother don't even live together, what are you talking about?"

"It's a long story."

"I've got time. There's nothing waiting for me at home, so you might as well start talking. Tell me what's going on. Help me to understand. Please."

"Okay. But you can't try to change my mind. Agreed?"

"No, I'm not going to agree to that. Unless you tell me that David Watters is a serial killer or something else crazy like that I'm not going to stop believing that he's the perfect man for you. So cut the drama and just tell me, okay?"

"Okay. But just let me get the story out without interruption. Can you at least agree to that?"

Michelle nodded her head. "Now start talking."

Sarah took a moment to gather her thoughts. "My mother was twelve years old when she got pregnant with me and thirteen when I was born. She was raped by a neighbor who was arrested and sent to prison. Mom was mature for her age and my grandmother made her take care of me. Nana told her that since it wasn't her fault, she had nothing to be ashamed of.

"My mother worked hard to keep up in school and raise me at the same time. When she was a senior, she started working at one of the downtown restaurants where she made pretty good money in tips. The owner of the restaurant encouraged her to learn the business so after graduation she went to Columbus State and enrolled in their culinary program. She worked her way up to become the Sous Chef at the restaurant. In order to do that she had to be gone a lot. Fortunately, we lived with my grandmother and great-grandmother and I never felt neglected.

"When I was a junior in high school, Mom started catering on the side to have enough money to send me to college. You've never seen anyone so proud as Mom and Nana the day I walked across the stage. Looking back I realize how blessed I was to grow up with three generations of independent black women who proved that you didn't need a man to make it."

"I know I'm not supposed to interrupt," Michelle began, "but your grandmother and great-grandmother were obviously married at one time."

"Yeah, but when their husbands died, they never wanted to re-marry. They had Jesus and didn't need anybody else."

"What about your mom?"

"She's never been married," Sarah acknowledged.

"Does she feel the same way her mother and grandmother felt?"

"Not to the extreme they did. She dates occasionally, but *Miss Julia's* keeps her busy."

"Do you agree with their philosophy?"

"Yes and no. I don't need a man to take care of me. I make good money; I'm buying my house and all that. But I recognize that there are times when having a man to come home to would be wonderful. And I also recognize that since I don't date any man who would possibly be a threat to my independence, I sometimes wonder if I'll ever get married."

"And you think David would change all of that," Michelle concluded.

"I know he would."

"Why?"

"David's the type of man who doesn't date casually. He has a great sense of humor and likes to have fun, but he's very serious about dating. If I give him the go-ahead, he'll see that as a sign that I'm ready for a serious relationship."

"And..."

"If I get involved with David, my mother will be alone. She's my best friend and I love her with all my heart. I would never do anything to hurt her."

"What if she met someone and got serious about him?"

"That would be great," Sarah admitted, "but I don't think it's going to happen."

"Why not?"

"My mom is an attractive, vibrant woman and men have tried for years to date her, but she isn't interested. It would take one heck of a man to get her attention."

"But," Michelle persisted, "If your mom was involved with some-one, then you would date David?"

"It's still not that simple, Mimi."

"Now what?" Michelle sighed.

"I've been brushing David off for so long, I don't know if he's still interested."

"Uh-huh. I think he's still interested. I see the way he looks at you. I bet if you gave him some type of sign, he would accept."

"I can't do that! The last thing I want is for him to think I'm run-ning after him."

"David is not going to think that about you."

"I just don't know. I've given him so many excuses whenever he's tried to set something up with just the two of us. I even told him I was too old for him."

"*What?*"

"Well, I am almost forty."

"And your point would be what?"

"He's only thirty-two."

"That's not so bad, Sarah. You need to stop making excuses and just go for it."

"I don't know Mimi..."

"I tell you what we're going to do. We're going to pray that God will send your mom a man who will knock her off her feet. Then we're going to pray for you and David. I just feel that the two of you were meant to be together and I'm going to ask God to work things out."

CHAPTER SEVENTEEN

Michelle put the finishing touches on a fresh floral arrangement just as the telephone rang.

"Hey, hey, Mimi. How ya doing?"

"Hey, David. What's going on with you?"

"A friend of mine is back in the States and I want you to come over to meet him."

"No," Michelle bluntly replied.

"No what?" David asked indignantly. "No, you can't come over here? No, you can't meet my friend? What?"

"No, I don't want to meet your friend."

"You don't even know anything about him."

"That's why I don't want to meet him."

"Listen, you need a social life. All work and no play will make Mimi very dull and boring."

"I have a very active social life, thank you very much," Michelle said in her own defense.

"With men?"

"I've got you."

"Yes you do. And we're very good friends, Mimi. But that's all we'll ever be." Michelle quickly figured out there would never be anything between them other than friendship and she was okay with that. Friendship with a man was a new concept for her, but she found that she truly enjoyed her relationship with David. "Don't you want to get married some day?"

"Sure."

"And how do you think that's going to happen if you never date?"

"I don't know. Maybe God will just deliver my husband to my door," Michelle said flippantly.

"And maybe He'll use your friend David to introduce you to a nice man," David retorted.

"Maybe."

"I'm not saying he's the one God has for you. All I know is G's good people and I think you will enjoy meeting him. Okay?"

"I don't know. I hate blind dates."

"It's not a blind date. It's me introducing you to one of my friends."

"But I don't know anything about him."

"But you know me, Michelle. I'm telling you, this brother is cool. He's saved, sanctified, has a good job..."

"He sounds too good to be true."

"...And he's a nice man. I think you'll enjoy meeting him if you give it a chance."

"Why don't you introduce him to Sarah?"

"Because I want to introduce him to you. Come on, Mimi."

"Oh, all right." Michelle finally gave in. She knew that David would keep hounding her so she might as well give in and meet the man.

"Well, don't sound so excited."

"Sarcasm doesn't become you, David. I'm not trying to be difficult. It's just awkward being set up like this."

"You're not being set up. How many times do I have to tell you?" David said in frustration. "Girl, you give new meaning to the word stubborn! He's a nice man and you're going to enjoy meeting him. Who knows? You two may take one look at each other, fall madly in love, get married and live happily ever after."

"Yeah, right!"

"Just don't forget to invite me to the wedding," David teased.

"I'm not going there with you." Michelle couldn't help laughing at David's antics.

"Okay! Okay!" David laughed. "Then are you coming over?"

"I don't want to go to your house. Why don't you come over here? But you've got to promise me that when I give you the signal, you'll both leave. Okay?"

"No problem," David agreed. "We'll be there by six. Hey, do you have any of those little puff things in the freezer?" Sarah's mother, Julia, occasionally shared her catering leftovers with Michelle.

"Yeah," Michelle replied. "I suppose you want me to fix them for you." David couldn't boil water which was surprising since he loved to eat.

"Well, if you insist," David innocently replied. "You know I'm still growing and need to keep my strength up."

Laughing, Michelle responded, "Yeah, right. I'll see you shortly." What have I gotten myself into? Michelle wondered as she hung up the phone. It hadn't been that long since her last disastrous date and now she was being set up on a blind date.

Michelle took inventory of her freezer. If David's friend ate as much as he did, crab puffs wouldn't be enough. Michelle took out stuffed potato skins and chicken wings. Thank God for Miss Julia's cooking. Michelle put everything in the oven and went to change clothes.

CHAPTER EIGHTEEN

The doorbell and the oven timer rang at the same time. Michelle ran to the kitchen to turn off the oven and reached the door just as the bell rang a second time. She opened the door and looked into the face of a man she hadn't seen in almost twelve years.

"Michael?"

"Michelle?"

"You two know each other?" David asked as he and Michael came into the house.

"Yes," they both responded simultaneously and then burst out laughing.

Michelle extended her hand. "Sienna Michelle Nickelson. Mimi to my friends."

Michael accepted her hand and shook it briefly. "Gregory Michael Stephens," Michael said as he slipped out of his leather jacket. "It's nice to see you again."

"Sienna?" inquired David cautiously.

"Yeah, silly. That's my first name. You knew that."

"No I didn't."

"I'm sure you did. You must have forgotten, but that's okay. Nobody ever called me Sienna but my mother. I'm Michelle or Mimi to everybody else." She noticed that Michael was holding his jacket. "Let me take your coat."

"I'll do it," David volunteered.

"Then come in and sit down, Michael. I just need to finish up in the kitchen and I'll be right back."

"Do you need any help?" Michael offered.

"No, I'll just be a minute. Have a seat and relax," Michelle said. She looked at Michael and shook her head, "What a small world."

"It sure is," agreed David, obviously distracted. He hung their jackets in the hall closet and returned to the living room just as Michelle came in from the kitchen.

"Hey, man, you okay?"

"Yeah, yeah. Just thinking about something," David muttered. He waited until Michelle sat down before continuing. "So it's obvious that you two know each other, huh?"

"We met...what...about twelve years ago?" Michael replied as he settled on the couch.

"On my eighteenth birthday."

"And the day after my mother's funeral. I needed to get out of the house and went to the mall. I met Michelle there. I told you about that, man. Don't you remember?"

"Yeah, vaguely," David replied. "There was a lot going on that week. Your mom's funeral, and that killer test in organic chemistry. Man, Professor Murphy wouldn't excuse me so I had to be in class the day after the funeral."

"They said that because she wasn't a relative you couldn't be excused," Michael remembered.

"Yeah, that was messed up. I spent more time at your house than I did mine."

"So I went to the mall and met Michelle, or Mimi as you call her," Michael continued.

David shook his head. "It really is a small world."

"So what happened to you? The last time I saw you, you were going to call me the next day," Michelle blurted.

"I called you the same day because I couldn't wait to talk to you again. You father told me that you couldn't be bothered and not to call back."

"You're kidding!"

"I kid you not." Michael still remembered her father's words although he would never repeat them to her.

"Oh, my goodness, I am so embarrassed."

"Don't be. I knew it was just him talking. I wrote you a couple of times, but the letters were returned unopened."

"I never knew," Michelle sadly responded. "I just thought I must have been boring and you were just being polite."

"I'm never that polite," Michael arrogantly replied. "I thought of you often."

"I've thought of you, too," Michelle confessed.

Trying to get a grip on his emotions, David interjected, "So I guess you won't be giving me a signal, huh?"

"What signal?" asked Michael.

"She insisted that we come over here and if she gave me the signal, we would leave."

"You didn't want to meet me?" Michael teased.

"I didn't know it was you. David called you "G." And even if he had called you Michael, I wouldn't have put you two together. We met in Cleveland. How could I know I would see you again in Columbus? Besides, the signal was going to be my safeguard."

"That makes sense. I'm glad you won't need it tonight."

CHAPTER NINETEEN

Michael couldn't believe how God had brought Michelle back into his life. He couldn't quite get the hang of thinking of her as Mimi, although he liked the nickname. He had to call his father and let him know about this new turn of events. Michael wasn't exaggerating when he told Michelle he had often thought of her. Whenever he did, he would pray for her and asked God to let him see her again. He had enough faith to believe that God would answer his prayer. Who knew God would answer it today? Michael hopped into the passenger seat of David's Navigator. "Man, I can't believe how God works."

"Uh-huh," David mumbled as he started the truck and backed into the street.

"I mean, I always knew I would see Michelle again, I just never knew when or where or how. But I just believed."

"Uh-huh."

"She still looks good," Michael continued. He got lost in the memory of seeing her again after all these years. She was still pretty.

"You met her before." David said.

"Earth to David. I told you we met on her eighteenth birthday. What's wrong with you?"

"We know her G."

"Of course we do. You know her from church and I met her twelve years ago."

"No man. We met her before that," David insisted.

"You're crazy. If I had met that woman, I would have remembered. She's pretty and funny and..."

"Man, listen to me," David responded emphatically. "We know her!"

"You better explain yourself, because I'm not sure I like where this conversation is going."

"Okay, man," David saw a fast food restaurant up ahead. "I'm going to pull in over there."

"This better be good," Michael warned.

David backed his truck into a slot at the far end of the parking lot and gripped the steering wheel. "Listen G. Do you remember the day we found that girl who had been attacked?"

"I'll never forget that. She was so little and blood was everywhere. All these years later, I still pray for her whenever she comes to mind."

"Me too, man."

"I've often wondered what happened to that little girl."

"Yeah, me too." David took a deep breath and voiced his suspicions. "I think that girl is Mimi."

"Get outta here! That's not the same girl."

"I think it is. That day we didn't know what we were doing, whether to leave her there, call the police, take her to the hospital, try to find her parents or what."

"Yeah, I remember. So?"

"We finally decided to just take her to the hospital ourselves."

"Yeah..."

"Well, you picked her up and started running to the hospital and I picked up her book bag. I thought it might have her name or something in it. I saw her ID tag and it said Sienna something, I can't remember the last name. Anyway, I didn't have time to see anything else because you had gotten so far ahead of me. Man, you were making good time."

"I was scared." Michael confessed.

"Yeah, me to. So I started praying and running. Good thing it happened in the neighborhood."

"Good?"

"You know what I mean. The hospital wasn't that far away."

"Oh, yeah."

"We came through those doors like something you see on TV and the nurse took over," David remembered.

"She pushed us out of the way and wouldn't tell us anything because we weren't related."

"That was messed up. I gave the nurse the book bag and I guess she called her parents."

"And the police. Can you believe they thought we attacked her and then felt guilty enough to bring her to the hospital? How crazy was that?" Michael was indignant all over again just from the memory.

"Well, you did have blood all over your shirt."

"Well, yeah, but…"

"I know G. Believe me I know." They both had more than their share of being racially profiled.

"So that's why you think Michelle is that girl?"

"That and the fact that her mom called my house the next day to thank me."

"I remember you telling me that. She told you to thank me for saving her daughter's life."

"Right. And her mom called her Sienna."

"I don't know, man. I'm still not convinced."

"I am G. Sienna is an unusual name and I've never forgotten it. When Mimi said her full name, it made the hair on my head stand up."

"You don't have any hair on your head," Michael reminded David.

"You know what I mean. I'm telling you that's the same girl."

"I'm not sure. She doesn't even look the same."

"Of course she doesn't!" David shot Michael an exasperated look. "Don't be dense. That girl was about twelve or thirteen. I think Michelle's about thirty. And, don't forget, that little girl's face was bloody and swollen."

"I don't know, man."

"Well, I do." David was convinced he was right. Besides, his gut hadn't failed him yet and his gut was telling him that he was on target with Michelle's identity. "Hey, since we're here do you want something from the drive-thru?"

"Man, you just ate at Michelle's house."

"Those little puff things and chicken wings? I'm still growing and I need real food. You know, a double cheeseburger and some fries."

"Yeah, you're growing all right."

"But I still look good," David smugly responded.

"Man, just order me a large coffee and take me home. I've got a lot to think about."

A few minutes later, Michael threw his keys on the table and sat on the couch, the coffee forgotten. Michelle couldn't be the same girl they found that day, could she? David was usually on target, and he had learned to trust his friend's instincts over the years, but he didn't know if he could get with him on this one.

Michael laid his head back and closed his eyes. He smiled as he remembered his first glimpse of Michelle that day in the mall. He then remembered his first glimpse of the little girl who had been attacked. She was a mess.

Michael wasn't convinced that Michelle was the same girl they found years ago, but he knew her home life couldn't have been that great. He remembered his own encounter with her father. Michael politely asked about Michelle's father earlier in the evening and she told him that he died a few years ago.

Michael couldn't do anything about Michelle's past. He could, however, do everything in his power to make sure she had a pleasant future.

CHAPTER TWENTY

Michelle found a comfortable spot on her sofa and hit the speed dial on her telephone. "Hey, Sarah, whatcha doing?"

"Trying to decide if I want to start grading term papers or not. You would think college kids would be more articulate, but that's not the case."

"I hear you, Dr. Caldwell, and I don't envy you at all. That goes with the territory of university life."

"Yeah, you're right. So what's up with you?"

"You are not going to believe what happened!"

"Whatever it is must be something good. I can feel your excitement coming through the phone. Tell me what happened."

"Okay, I'll try." Michelle knew she needed to calm down or she'd never get the story out. She took a deep breath, let it out slowly and began talking. "Earlier today David called and invited me to his house to introduce me to one of his friends."

"And knowing you the way I do, it was probably like pulling teeth, wasn't it?" Sarah teased.

"Not quite, but close," Michelle laughed. "I told David to introduce him to you, but he wasn't having it." Michelle paused to see if Sarah would respond to her teasing, but she didn't. "Anyway, I finally decided to have them come over, but I told David if I gave him a sign both of them were to leave. I wasn't in the mood to be bothered with another man still hung up on his ex-wife, you know."

"Yeah, I know. And I also know you had to fix David something to eat, didn't you?" Sarah laughed.

"You know I did, girl! That man can put away some food. Fortunately I had some stuff in the freezer that your mom had given me so I just threw it in the oven and made some punch."

"So what happened?"

"I have to start at the beginning. On my eighteenth birthday I met this really nice man named Michael Stephens at the mall who was home from college. We talked and had ice cream. Then he walked me home and said he was going to call me, but he never did."

"Bummer!"

"Yeah," Michelle agreed. "Over the years I would occasionally think about him, but I didn't think I would never see him again. Well tonight he was the friend David wanted to introduce me to."

"You're kidding!" Sarah exclaimed.

"The same man, girl! I can't believe it!"

"Did he recognize you?"

"Yeah, we both recognized each other at the same time and started laughing and David thought we were crazy. It turns out that he called me the same day we met, but my father wouldn't let him talk to me."

"Oh, Mimi. That's too bad."

"And he said he wrote me, but the letters kept getting returned. I never knew any of this, Sarah. If my father weren't already dead, I would give him a piece of my mind, parent or no parent."

"Don't go there."

"You're right. Let me just focus on what's happening now. The past is the past and there's nothing that can be done about it."

"Good attitude. So tell me about this man. How old is he?"

"He's thirty-two."

"And what does he look like?"

"Gorgeous. He's tall, probably about six two or three, well-built with broad shoulders. Actually he looks exactly the same except he has a goatee now instead of just a mustache. He has this killer smile and perfect white teeth. And get this. He even has dimples."

"Dimples?"

"Yeah, girl," Michelle laughed. "God was in a real good mood the day He created him."

"I hear you! So what does he do?"

"I have no idea." Michelle realized she never found out anything personal about Michael. "David said that he just moved back to the

States, but I didn't think to ask him where he had been or what he did for a living."

"So what did the three of you do?"

"Well, you know David's always the entertainer. They were only here for a couple of hours and they kept me rolling with stories about college and stuff. They both seem to have a strange sense of humor, which is probably why they're friends."

"Did he ask to see you again?"

"No, but he asked for my phone number and said he would call."

"That's good," Sarah offered hopefully.

"Yeah."

"I'll be praying for you. There must be a reason God let you meet this man again. We'll just have to trust Him until He reveals the reason."

"I know that's right. I never thought I would see Michael again, but when he showed up tonight it was like we were never apart. Funny, huh?"

"I know you're excited about seeing him again, Mimi, but try to keep things in perspective. Don't jump ahead of God, okay?" Sarah cautioned.

"I won't."

CHAPTER TWENTY-ONE

Michelle had thought of Michael every once in a while, but never in her wildest imagination would she have believed that God would have Michael standing on her doorstep with a former co-worker. The ringing telephone surprised her. "Hello."

"Hi, Michelle, it's Michael. Were you asleep?"

"Almost."

"I won't keep you then. I wanted to tell you I had a good time tonight. When David said he wanted me to meet a friend of his, I had no idea God would bring you back into my life. And to think I almost didn't come. Hey, do you still like ice cream?" Michael asked.

"Sure do."

"Did you have your nightly bowl?"

"I can't believe you remember that!" Michelle was impressed.

"I remember a lot about that day," Michael responded softly.

"I do, too."

"Would you like to go out for ice cream sometime?"

"Yes."

"Tomorrow?"

"Sounds good. What time?"

"How about I pick you up around seven?"

"I'm looking forward to it."

"Me too. I'm glad I ran into you again. Thank God for David."

"I agree. Goodnight."

"Sweet dreams, Michelle."

CHAPTER TWENTY-TWO

MAY 21

Michelle rushed in from work and had just enough time to shower and change. Fortunately she had already decided on a simple outfit of black pants and a pale pink cashmere sweater. She was ready when the doorbell rang. "Hi, Michael. Come on in."

"You look very nice."

"Thank you. Can I take your jacket?" Michelle noticed that he looked good, too. He was wearing black jeans and a black silk tee shirt with a thin leather bomber jacket.

"No thanks." Michael extended a gift-wrapped box to Michelle. "I hope you like this."

"Thank you." Inside the box was a delicately carved crystal butterfly perched on a yellow rose. "It's beautiful, Michael."

"I noticed last night that you like butterflies so I wanted to contribute to the collection."

"This is so nice of you. I know exactly where to put it." Michelle placed the butterfly in the center of the mantle above the fireplace.

"How long have you been a collector?" Michael joined Michelle at the mantle.

"Since I was fourteen."

"Why butterflies?"

"Because they represent new beginnings. You know the metamorphous of changing from an ugly caterpillar into a beautiful butterfly and then flying away."

"Freedom?" Michael guessed.

"Yes, freedom." Michelle was amazed at his perception.

"Then I'm glad I chose this." Michael smiled down at Michelle. "I found this in a small gift store when I was in China. I didn't understand why I bought it until I saw your collection."

"China?"

"I lived there for two years and returned home about six months ago."

"What were you doing there?"

"I was working for a financial planning and investment company and was assigned to handle one of their accounts in China. It took a few months to adjust to being there, but I eventually learned a few phrases in Chinese and started enjoying the adventure. We don't always understand why God opens certain doors, but we need to be ready to walk through them."

"Amen."

"Anyway, while I was there, I knew when I returned home I would be ready to strike out on my own. I started saving money while in college for the day I would be my own boss. With the bonus money I received from the China experience, I have enough to get started."

"So what do you do now?"

"I handle various aspects of financial planning, investing, managing and advising. Basically a jack of all trades when it comes to money."

"That sounds interesting."

"It is. Are you ready to go?"

"Sure. I'm always ready for ice cream."

CHAPTER TWENTY-THREE

Michael led Michelle to a corner table in the food court's open floor plan. "How's this?"

"Fine, Michael."

"Would you like something other than ice cream?"

"No thanks. I had a late lunch."

"So what flavor will it be tonight? Butter pecan, strawberry, peach..." Michael teased.

"You're hilarious. I think I'll have peach."

"One serving of peach ice cream coming up. I'll be right back."

Michelle watched him walk away and couldn't help but admire the way he looked in those jeans, and then admonished herself for noticing. Slow down girl she cautioned herself. She didn't know what the reason was for God allowing Michael back in her life, but she knew she didn't want to mess up whatever the plan was. Celibacy hadn't been an issue since salvation because she hadn't been physically attracted to anyone. But, her hormones had been going crazy since last night, and she understood why. Everything about Michael Stephens was sexy—his height, built, personality and that great voice. Michelle remembered the first time she heard that sexy voice of his. If anything it was now deeper and it still made her stomach flutter. Sweet dreams indeed! Oh, yeah, she was really going to have to stay prayed up! Michelle saw Michael walking back toward her and tried to reign in her thoughts. "I see you got your banana split. Do you think you have enough cherries on top?" It was Michelle's turn to tease Michael.

"Yes. There can never be too many cherries on a banana split." Michael took a large bite of his ice cream. "This is good. How's yours?"

"Delicious. This place makes the best ice cream in the city."

"Good. So tell me about you. What have you been doing since the last time I saw you?"

"That was just a few hours ago."

"Cute. You know what I mean. What have you been doing since the very first time we talked?"

"Too much to try to fit into one evening."

"Then I guess we'll just have to get together again won't we?" Michael confidently asked.

"Absolutely!"

Michael nodded his head. "So tell me about you. What do you do?"

"Well, I did go to Tri-C and received my Associate's Degree. Then I moved to Columbus, transferred to Franklin University and did my Bachelor's and MBA. During the last year of my master's program I started working in the same building David does and three years ago I started my own consulting firm."

"Good for you. What type of consultant are you?"

"My company specializes in non-profit operations. We're a full service company offering grant writing, grant administration and every-thing in between," Michelle proudly responded.

"How many employees do you have?"

"I have a full-time staff of three and several consultants who work on a contractual basis."

"Do you enjoy your work?"

"Very much. I was never happy working for someone else, but I used that experience to my advantage before stepping out on my own."

"I hear you. I worked in every possible area of the company be-fore I left. Some of my co-workers thought I was crazy, but I knew that I would need to have practical experience as well as book knowledge. That's one of the reasons I accepted the assignment to China. It wasn't just about the money. It was part of the plan to be successful when I struck out on my own."

"You're right. The challenges of self-employment can be over-whelming sometimes, but I know that God told me to do this. And as long as I stay in His will, I know I can overcome any challenge."

"Amen, sister. But the rewards outweigh the challenges."

"Exactly. I love the flexibility of being self-employed, but more importantly I love the satisfaction of knowing I'm helping my non-profits stay on track."

Michael grabbed both of their jackets and suggested they walk around the mall once they finished their ice cream.

"Are you trying to recreate our first meeting?"

"You catch on quick," Michael said as he winked at Michelle. "Are you okay with that?"

"Sure."

"We'll walk around the mall, talk some more and this time I'll drive you home, okay?" Michael held his hand out.

"Okay." Michelle slipped her hand into Michael's.

"Did you ever get married?"

"No. What about you?"

Michael hesitated before shaking his head. "I guess I never found the right woman."

"You must meet plenty of women in your work and travels," Michelle prompted.

"I didn't say I didn't meet women. I said I never found the right woman. Don't get me wrong, I'm a healthy heterosexual man. I just haven't found the woman God has created specifically for me."

"Do you really believe that?"

"What? That God creates one person specifically for another?"

"Yes."

"Yes, I do. I think that each of us has a soul mate or life mate, if you will, created from the foundation of the world. I just haven't found her yet or God hasn't revealed her to me yet. When He does, I'll make my move and sweep her off her feet."

"Sweep her off her feet, huh?"

"Yeah. What about you? Any serious relationships?"

"Not really."

"Come on. A woman who looks like you and with your intelligence must have men hitting on her all the time."

"That doesn't mean I'm interested."

"You're right. I'm sorry. I shouldn't assume anything," Michael smiled at her in apology. "You said that you and David worked in the same building. Is that where you met?"

"Yes. We worked for different companies. There weren't a lot of minorities in the building so we basically all knew each other," Michelle paused to chuckle. "He kept trying to get me saved."

"That sounds just like him. It must have worked because he said you're very active at church."

"I am now. He invited me to church and six years ago I went, gave my life to the Lord and have been at the Christian Center ever since."

"Good."

"What about you? How did you and David meet?"

"We were seven years old and some of the kids from the neighborhood were making fun of me because I was adopted. He and another boy named Terrance stood up for me. Terrance was three years older than we were, but we all became best friends. David and I went through school together and even did our master's programs together. Terrance and David were the closest things I had to brothers."

"You're adopted?"

"Yes."

"But the first day I met you was the day after your mother's funeral. Was that your adopted mother or biological mother, if you don't mind my asking?"

"I don't mind. You can ask me anything you like," Michael paused to squeeze Michelle's hand. "I never knew my biological mother. I have a biological sister who's a year older than me, and I think she remembers a little bit about our mother. As far as I know, we were just abandoned one day and ended up in the foster care system until I was seven and she was eight. That's when our parents adopted us."

"Is your father still alive?"

"Yes. He's a semi-retired CPA and lives in Shaker Heights."

"What about your sister?"

"She lives in Dallas. Brianna and her husband Calvin have three kids, Calvin Jr., Amanda and Daniel. I see them about twice a year, but we talk often and, of course, keep in touch through e-mail."

"So David was your protector, huh?"

"Yeah, he's a great guy. We were inseparable. If you saw one of us, you saw the other. David, Terrance and I were the Three Musketeers. We all gave our lives to Christ when we were teenagers."

"Does Terrance live in Columbus?"

"I don't know. We lost touch over a dozen years ago. It was like one day he was there and the next he wasn't. I still see his father, but he's lost touch with him, too. I just pray that he's okay. It's been a long time since I've seen him."

Michelle decided to lighten up the conversation as they walked to Michael's truck. "What did David tell you about me?"

"He said you were a nice woman who needed to meet a good brother."

"Didn't he describe me?"

"Not really."

"Oh, I thought that's why you weren't interested in coming over that night."

"You're kidding, right?" Michael shook his head at the unlikelihood of her statement. "I wasn't interested because I was tired. I had been burning the candle at both ends working on a presentation for a potential client. I told David I could meet you another time, but he was so insistent."

"I know what you mean. So what if I had been unattractive?" She coyly asked. Michelle was pleased to see that her flirting skills hadn't totally rusted.

"It wouldn't have mattered. Don't get me wrong. I was very pleased when you opened the door, especially once I realized who you were. But I didn't come over to meet a potential girlfriend; I came to meet a sister in the Lord. What about you? Did David describe me to you?"

"No."

"And...?" Michael was obviously fishing for a compliment.

"Oh, okay," Michelle smiled. "Yes, I was happy with what I saw. Satisfied?"

"Very much," Michael smiled in return.

Michael pulled into Michelle's driveway and came around to open her car door. He took her key, unlocked the front door and moved aside for her to precede him. "Did you have a good time?"

"Yes I did. You're fun company."

"Thank you. So we can do this again?

"Yes."

"Tomorrow?" Michael asked hopefully.

"Tomorrow?"

"Yeah, you know a few hours from now."

"Don't be a smart aleck."

"Okay! Okay! Seriously, I want to see you again, Michelle, and the sooner the better. I'm not trying to rush you, though. It's just that now that you're back in my life, I would like to see where this leads. How does that sound?"

"I would like that, too."

"Michelle, will you give me the pleasure of your company at dinner tomorrow night?" Michael formally asked.

"Yes."

"Good. I'll pick you up at eight. I have to go to Cincinnati in the morning, but I should be back around six. I'll take you someplace fancy to make up for the ice cream."

"I enjoyed the ice cream, but dinner would be nice."

"Good."

"Would you like to come in for coffee?"

"Not tonight. I have to be on the road early. Rain check?"

"Of course."

"I had a very nice time tonight." Michael wrapped his arms around Michelle, gave her a brief squeeze and kissed her on the cheek. "I'll see you tomorrow."

"Goodnight."

Michelle found herself humming as she set the alarm, turned off the lights and went to bed.

CHAPTER TWENTY-FOUR

AUGUST 19

Michelle placed a sweet potato pie on the counter and reached for dessert plates and forks. She and Michael had been out for pizza and bowling to celebrate their three month anniversary and they were sitting at her kitchen counter waiting for coffee to brew.

"Do you like children?" Michael suddenly asked.

"Very much."

"Have you thought of having any?"

Michael saw the brief flash of sadness that crossed Michelle's face before she answered, "Sure."

"How many?" Michael persisted.

"Hmm. Let me think about this. I know I don't want an only child like I am, so maybe two or three."

"How do you feel about adoption?"

"Why are you asking me these questions?"

"I'm just interested in how you feel about children. So how do you feel about adoption?"

"Honestly? I've never thought about it one way or the other. I don't think I'm opposed to it. You're adopted and you turned out okay," Michelle teased.

"Yeah, but those early years were rough. It was unusual for one family to adopt two kids at the same time, but Mom and Dad didn't want to split us up."

"Praise God!"

"Amen to that."

"So, what about you, Michael?" Michelle figured two could play the game. "Do you like kids? Do you want your own someday?"

"I love kids. I get a kick out of spoiling my niece and nephews. But I would have to adopt."

"Really? Why?"

"I'm sterile."

"Sterile? As in you can't-make-a-woman-pregnant sterile?"

Michael nodded his head. "Remember when I said I was in the foster care system until I was seven?"

"Yes."

"I was behind on all of my shots by the time my parents adopted me. And then I caught the mumps when I was twenty-one and the doctor said I would probably be infertile."

"Oh, Michael."

"I always wanted to look at a child knowing he or she was created with the woman I love, but that evidently isn't God's plan for me. Don't get me wrong. It's easy to accept it now, but I was bummed out at first. And I'll confess that God and I had several heated discussions before I came to my senses and recognized His sovereignty. I believe I will make a good father and there are a lot of children just waiting to be adopted, so it's not that bad."

Michelle didn't know how to respond so she busied herself pouring their coffee and cutting the pie. When she sat back down, Michael gently traced the scar over her eyebrow. "How did this happen?"

Michelle thought about what to say and finally decided to tell the truth. After all, he'd been honest about his condition; she could be just as honest. "I was attacked and raped coming home from school when I was fourteen."

"Oh, honey. I'm so sorry."

"It's all right. It was a long time ago."

"But I hate that you were hurt."

"It was bad." Michelle agreed.

"Does it bother you to talk about it?"

"Not anymore. I had to have stitches in my forehead, which is where this scar came from, my nose and arm were broken and some teeth were knocked out. I had five separate surgeries as a result of the rape. If it weren't for the boys who brought me to the hospital, I probably would have died."

Michael had a suspicion that he knew where this conversation was headed. "Who were the boys that found you?" He cautiously asked.

"I don't know. As much as my mother could figure out, two older boys were coming home and found me in the bushes. One of them picked me up and carried me to the hospital. Fortunately, it was only a few blocks away. The doctor and my mother said they saved my life."

"Did they ever catch the guy who did it?"

"I don't think so, or if they did, I was never notified."

"Will you tell me what happened?"

"My friends and I would stop at Smithy's Market every day on the way home from school. Do you know it?"

"Yeah. Me and my boys would stop in sometimes after practice. They always had the coldest soda and the best hot wings."

"Yeah, I remember. Smithy's was our separation point; Maria and Stephanie went one way and I went the other. On this particular day there were a group of boys hanging across the street. They could have been anywhere from sixteen to twenty years old, I really didn't look at them and tried to ignore them when I walked past. The next thing I remember was waking up in the hospital. I was out of school for four months and had to take summer courses so I wouldn't fall behind."

"Do you think the boys on the corner attacked you?"

"I don't know. Even if they had, I didn't really look at them so I wouldn't have been able to tell the police anything. I just remembered that whoever raped me smelled like beer and cigarettes."

"How did you deal with all this? I mean did you have counseling or anything like that?"

"Not right away. My father didn't believe in airing dirty laundry as he called it, so I didn't get any help. I shied away from boys for a while. Actually the day I met you was the first time I willingly had a conversation with a boy alone."

"I was that persuasive, huh?"

"No, you were that persistent." Michelle poked Michael in the arm with her finger. "Anyway, back to your question about counseling. It wasn't until after I was saved that I realized I needed help to deal with the attack. I asked my friend Sarah Caldwell about counselors and she introduced me to one of the professors from the college who also had a private practice. She helped me understand a lot about the attack and work through my anger."

"Good."

"Because of her and the Lord I was able to forgive my attacker. It was hard, but I knew it was necessary if I was going to be able to move on."

CHAPTER TWENTY-FIVE

SEPTEMBER 6

Michelle was anxious for the clock to reach a decent hour before calling. A female voice groggily answered the telephone on the third ring and Michelle immediately started talking. "Hey, Nikki. The Lord woke me up early this morning thinking about you. Are you okay?"

"Don't start with that Jesus stuff, Mimi. Just because I went to church with you a couple of times doesn't mean I want you calling me up with the spooky stuff."

"It's not spooky. It's spiritual." Nikki's aversion to church wasn't anything new. She had made several veiled comments about a bad experience, but she never elaborated and Michelle never pressed. "So how are you?"

"I've been better."

"You don't sound good," Michelle agreed. "Do you feel okay?"

"I'm pregnant."

"What? How? Well, I know how, but..."

"I know. How did this happen?

"Yeah."

"It just did. You know I don't go nowhere without my supply of condoms."

"I remember."

"A few weeks ago I met this guy named Terry at the club and one thing led to another. Things happened so fast that we ended up doing it in the back seat of his car. I was so high I wasn't thinking about condoms or much of anything else."

"Oh, Nikki."

"I know. Don't even say it." Nikki sounded so miserable. "But you know what the funny thing is?"

"What?"

"When it came time for him to … uh…release, if you know what I mean…"

"I do."

"I knew we had made a baby. It was like I could feel the sperm finding the egg and life being created."

"Have you told the father?"

"No. I can't get in touch with him," Nikki sniffed. "The number he gave me belongs to someone else and I don't have his address. As much as I hate to admit this, I don't even know his last name."

"So what are you going to do?"

"Have an abortion."

"*No!* Nikki, you can't do that."

"I can and I will. Girl, this is the twenty-first century. I can have an abortion as easy as going to have a tooth pulled."

"I know, but please Nikki. I'm begging you. Don't do this."

"Mimi, I can't have a baby. I'm up for promotion at the bank. I'm too young. I can't be bothered with a baby."

"Then you should have thought about that before having unprotected sex in the back seat of a car with a man you just met!" Michelle angrily retorted.

"What do you know about it?" Nikki snapped back. "Since you've been saved, you've turned into a goody two-shoes."

"And you know better than most people that I haven't always been saved," Michelle responded just as heatedly. "We were in the streets together. So don't talk to me like I don't know what's going on. I know more about this than you think."

"Yeah, right," Nikki snorted.

"Yeah, right! I had an abortion and it was the most horrible experience of my life." Michelle hadn't planned on sharing that information with anyone, but as soon as the words left her mouth she knew that was why God had her call Nikki.

"What?" Nikki asked in surprise. "When?"

"It happened when I was nineteen. I was raped when I was fourteen. And I know my father always blamed me. We never had a great relationship even before the rape and after the rape it just got crazier.

Whenever I would go out of the house, he would always make some snide remark about not coming home pregnant or dressing like a slut or something else mean. When my mother died, he became ten times worse.

"The funny thing was that after the rape, I never talked to boys unless there were a lot of people around, and I never dressed like a slut. I wore clothes that were at least a size too big just so no one would notice my shape. But it wasn't enough. The one time I did talk to a boy, he said he would call and didn't."

Caught up in the retelling, Michelle was unaware that tears were running down her face. "I moved out of the house when I graduated from high school and shared an apartment with Maria and Stephanie while I went to Tri-C. Right before I graduated, I started dating one of the associate professors. Brian had been flirting with me most of the year so I decided to take him up on his offer. He said all the things I had always wanted to hear and turned my head with his words of love. You know the drill. I thought I was in love, but I was just stupid. He was the first man I willingly gave myself to.

"I found out I was pregnant and that Brian was married in the same week. He told me in no uncertain terms that he wouldn't support the baby and had the nerve to question whether it was even his. He made sure I also understood that he wasn't going to leave his wife. To make a long story short, I didn't feel like I had a lot of options." Michelle paused to gather her composure.

"All I could hear was my father's voice in my head calling me a slut. I knew that if I kept the baby I would have to hear "I told you so" and I realized that I would have fulfilled his low expectations of me. I made the worst mistake of my life by having the abortion. It was a horrible, horrible experience both physically and emotionally. Please reconsider doing this or you'll regret it for the rest of your life. I know I do. Whenever I see a child about the age mine would be, I always wonder what would have happened if I kept the child. Nikki, I know what I'm talking about. Don't do this to yourself."

"I never knew, Mimi."

"No one did except Maria and Stephanie."

"How have you coped with it?"

"It wasn't easy. When I was in the world, I dealt with the guilt by sleeping around, drinking and doing drugs. Anything to escape the memories, you know? Once I got saved, Sarah introduced me to a Christian counselor who helped me deal with the rape. I talked to the counselor about the abortion and the guilt and she walked me through the whole forgiveness process."

"What forgiveness process?"

"Well, I had to forgive the baby's father for not standing by me. But more importantly, I had to forgive myself. The Bible tells us that God casts our sin in the sea of forgetfulness. I asked Him to forgive me and I believe He did. But I had a harder time forgiving myself for taking things into my own hands. You're the fourth person I've ever told about the abortion. I believe God wanted me to share with you so that you wouldn't make the same mistake. It's just not worth the heartache."

"Listen, Mimi. This is too much for me. I'll think about it, but I'm not making any promises one way or the other. But I will think about it."

"Okay, that's all I'm asking." Michelle hung up and fell to her knees. She asked God to watch over Nikki and help her make the right decision. She also asked God to help her deal with the repercussions of telling her about the abortion. Michelle hadn't planned on sharing that episode of her life with anyone else; obviously God had other plans.

CHAPTER TWENTY-SIX

SEPTEMBER 20

Michelle sat in a tub of lavender-scented bubbles and let the tears freely cascade down her face. She was going to have to let Michael go and it was going to break her heart. She loved him. She didn't know why it hadn't occurred to her until then that what she felt for Michael was love but there it was. She was in love with him and she was going to have to let him go.

After Michelle told Nikki about the abortion, she realized she was going to have to tell Michael, too. It would be the right thing to do. She couldn't take a chance on him finding out through someone else. But she knew that telling Nikki was what God wanted her to do. She hadn't heard from Nikki since that phone call, but kept praying that she would do the right thing. She was going to have to tell the story again to Michael. And she didn't think he would be able to accept what she had done.

They had been together at least three times a week since the night he had come over with David. When they didn't see each other, they spent hours on the telephone. They went to the movies, bowling and football games, sometimes alone and sometimes with David, Sarah or other members of their church. They took long walks and had meals in fast food establishments and five-star restaurants. They went on picnics and read poetry. They went to the amusement park and discovered their mutual love of roller coasters. They drove to Cleveland often to visit his father who was an older version of Michael. It was hard to believe Donavon wasn't his biological father because they looked so much alike, even down to the dimples. On one of their visits, she had a chance to meet Brianna and her family. She and Brianna became instant friends and e-mailed or texted one another often. Michelle loved Michael's family.

The tears fell harder and the memories came faster. On their first real date, Michael arrived wearing a black suit and a pristine white French cuffed shirt. He looked great! The red in his tie perfectly matched the straight sheath Michelle had chosen and they laughed at how coordinated they were. He took her to a cozy downtown spot where they ate crab cakes and listened to smooth jazz. They shared their first kiss that night standing just inside her front door. It was everything she imagined it would be.

Over these past few months, they had talked about every subject imaginable. They knew how each other felt about sex (not until the wedding night), tithing (absolutely), politics (they both voted Independent), sports (he loved football; she liked basketball) and debt-free living (both in favor). They both had excellent credit ratings and were each buying their homes, although Michelle lived in a condo.

They had even talked about the uncomfortable subject of sexual histories. Michelle admitted having been sexually active before salvation and that she took a HIV test every six months to be sure she was still negative. She hadn't been celibate long enough to be worry-free about the virus. Michelle discovered that Michael was a virgin.

On subjects they didn't agree on like pets (he liked them, she didn't) and foreign versus American cars (she drove a BMW 725i; Michael drove a Ford Expedition), they respected the other's opinion. Michael was every bit as wonderful as he appeared to be the day she first met him. How was she going to let him go? Why would God bring him back into her life to tease her with what could have been?

Michelle had already decided she was going to tell him tonight. She had put it off as long as she could. She and Michael planned to have dinner together and it was her turn to cook. That was something else they had in common. They both loved good food and were both excellent cooks, although Michael was more of a gourmet than Michelle. Sniffling, Michelle couldn't stop the memories. The first meal Michael cooked for her was beef enchiladas with a red sauce that almost took the top of her head off. She loved them! Her first meal for him was more traditional—fried chicken, potato salad, greens and yeast rolls made from scratch. She discovered his love of brownies and he discovered her love of lemon meringue pie.

Michelle had to stop crying. She wanted to look her best for Michael tonight and it was hard to be cute with puffy eyes. She wrapped herself in a terry cloth robe and went into her dressing room. She thumbed through the closet until she found just what she was looking for—a rose colored raw silk sleeveless pantsuit with a sweetheart neckline. She would wear her hair down and make sure her makeup was perfect. She was preparing Michael's favorite dinner of grilled salmon, roasted red skin potatoes and asparagus with hollandaise sauce. Now all she had to do was get through the night.

CHAPTER TWENTY-SEVEN

Dinner went better than Michelle expected. Michael kept the conversation going, although she caught his concerned look more than once. She sent him to the living room while she cleared the dishes after declining his invitation to help. Michelle started the dishwasher, gave the counter a final swipe and put the towel aside. Putting off taking to Michael wasn't going to make things any easier. The coffee finished brewing and she poured it into a carafe. She placed cups, spoons, cream and sugar on a tray and headed for the living room.

Michael was sitting on the couch when she came in. She put the tray down and prepared a cup of coffee just the way she knew he liked it with light cream and two sugars. He thanked her as he accepted the cup and sat it on the table. "What's wrong, sweetheart. You've been quiet all evening."

Michelle poured her own coffee and carried it to the mantle over the unlit fireplace. She fingered the crystal butterfly Michael gave her almost five months ago and stared at the fireplace as if she could will it to change what had to be said. She heard Michael moving from the couch and knew that at any moment he was going to approach her. She couldn't allow that. If he touched her, she would fall apart. "I've enjoyed our time together Michael."

Hearing the past tense of the statement, Michael paused in his tracks. "Enjoyed?" Michael repeated softly.

Michelle took another ragged breath. "I can't see you anymore, Michael. I'm sorry."

Michael put his hands on her shoulders. "Michelle, what's going on? We've been together almost every night for the past five months. I deserve an answer."

"I had an abortion," whispered Michelle.

Wham! Michael felt the same way he did the first time he was tackled by a two hundred pound linebacker. All the air seemed to dissolve from his lungs and he felt faint. Had she cheated on him? While he was being respectful and treating her like the queen she is had she been seeing someone else? That couldn't be. She was too honorable of a woman to play two men against one another, wasn't she? Besides, they were together almost every night. When would she have had time for anyone else? Michael dismissed the idea of infidelity and knew that whatever he said now would affect the rest of their relationship. God, help me say the right thing, Michael silently prayed. "When did this happen?"

"When I was nineteen."

Michael relaxed and expelled the breath he'd been holding. It was going to be okay. Turning Michelle toward him, he was devastated by the anguish on her beautiful face. Not only had she gone through a traumatic experience, she thought he was going to walk away from her over something that occurred years before he met her. He couldn't blame her. Hadn't he thought she cheated on him?

Michael took Michelle's hand and led her to one of the chairs facing the fireplace. He pulled her down onto his lap and noticed the coolness of her skin. He jerked the cashmere throw from the other chair and wrapped it around her. "I'm sorry you went through something like that." Michael placed Michelle's head against his shoulder.

"Don't you want to know what happened? Or why I did it?" Michelle loved the feel of his arms around her.

"Only if you want to tell me." Michael kissed Michelle's forehead. "I'll listen to whatever you want to say."

His reaction was not at all what she expected. She thought he would end the relationship and instead he was offering comfort and understanding. Michelle closed her eyes and inhaled the scent of his citrus cologne. She gathered the strength to tell him everything about that horrible experience. She didn't realize she was crying until he wiped the tears away and that was her undoing. She turned her face in toward his neck and let loose with all the torment locked up inside. Michael rocked her gently in his arms and let her cry it out. Cry for the child she had lost. Cry for what might have been. Cry for the unfairness of life. He didn't try to stop her tears because she needed this.

And while she cried, he prayed. Michael knew God could help Michelle. Wasn't He the mender of broken hearts? When Michael realized that Michelle had fallen asleep, he carefully carried her to the couch. Poor baby. She had cried herself to sleep. Michael placed the throw over her and returned to the chair. So that's why she was so distant tonight. He couldn't begin to imagine what a woman went through making the decision to abort a child. Judging from Michelle's reaction, it was major. Her pain was still fresh, even all these years later. Michael prayed again for God to heal her. He knew that she would never be whole until she allowed the Lord to heal this hurt. It was under the blood, but Michael knew that sometimes it was harder to forgive your-self. Michael relaxed back in the chair, closed his eyes and waited for Michelle to wake up.

CHAPTER TWENTY-EIGHT

Michael opened his eyes several hours later to sunshine. He hadn't planned on falling asleep, but based on the stiffness in his body he had done just that. The clock read seven thirty but that couldn't be, could it?

He awkwardly got to his feet and tried to shake life back into his sleeping limbs. Michael stopped at the linen closet and helped himself to one of the new toothbrushes he knew that Michelle kept for guests. He also took a wash cloth and towel and headed for the bathroom.

On the way back to the kitchen, Michael slipped into the living room and removed the tray from last night. Michelle was in the same position that he placed her in the night before. He made a fresh pot of coffee and opened the cupboard to determine what he would cook for breakfast. He was hungry and knew that Michelle had to be, too, since she'd only picked over her food last night. Michael discovered all the ingredients for quiche and then smiled when he looked in the freezer. He knew he was a good cook, but pie crusts eluded him; he was glad Michelle kept a supply of frozen crusts on hand.

Michael sat at the counter and drank a cup of coffee. The quiche would take forty-five minutes to bake so he emptied the dishwasher and cleaned up his mess. He poured a fresh cup of coffee and headed for the living room. Michelle was just starting to stir when he walked in. "Good morning." Michael handed the cup to Michelle. "How do you feel?"

Michelle gratefully accepted the coffee. "Better. Thanks." She wasn't looking at him and Michael didn't think that was a good sign.

"Breakfast will be ready in about thirty minutes, so you have time to freshen up." Michael offered Michelle his hand to assist her off the couch. He knew she had to be stiff since the couch was designed for sitting, not sleeping.

"Thanks." Michelle practically ran to her bedroom. She was so embarrassed and couldn't believe what happened last night. She hadn't planned on falling asleep or Michael staying. What would her neighbors think about his truck in her driveway all night?

Michelle walked into the bathroom, glanced at her reflection in the mirror and almost hollered. Raccoon eyes! Not only had she cried like a baby while sitting on the man's lap, he saw her with mascara running down her face. Michael didn't seem to have any problem with her tears, but that didn't mean she was going to make a habit of falling apart around him.

Michelle took a quick shower and changed into jeans and a tee shirt. She pulled on a pair of crew socks and padded back to the kitchen. Whatever Michael was cooking smelled delicious and Michelle realized she was starving. "Whatever that is smells heavenly."

Michael was just pulling something out of the oven. "I hope it tastes as good as it smells. And I also hope you like quiche." Michael smiled in her direction.

"I do, although I very seldom make it. It's hard to just make enough for one or two servings and that's usually all I want." Michelle knew she was rambling but couldn't help it.

Michael noticed that Michelle had yet to look at him, but that was about to change. "Michelle, look at me," Michael gently ordered standing directly in front of her.

When Michelle reluctantly lifted her gaze, Michael bent down and kissed her softly on the lips. "Thank you for sharing with me last night. I know it was hard for you. I'm glad you did."

"I had no choice. You needed to know."

"And you thought that because of something you did years before I met you that I would leave you?"

Michelle was momentarily distracted by the tear and makeup stains on Michael's shirt. She definitely owed him a new one. "I didn't know how you would react," Michelle admitted. "I think that most men would have left."

"I'm not most men."

"No, you're not. You're very special," Michelle reached up to kiss Michael on the side of his mouth. "Thank you."

"You're very welcome. Let's eat."

With plates of quiche and orange slices before them, Michael and Michelle took their time eating. The food was just as good as it smelled. Twenty minutes later, Michael asked, "So what's on your agenda for today?"

"Nothing." Michelle helped Michael clear the table. "My plan was to break up with you last night and spend today crying about it. I didn't make any other plans."

"I'm glad we're not breaking up." Michael started loading the dishwasher. "Since you're free, how about riding to Cleveland with me to see Dad?"

"Okay. I like your father."

"He likes you, too. Let me go home and change. I'll be back in a couple of hours and then we'll leave. We'll spend the day there and come back later tonight."

"Sounds good."

At the door, Michael took Michelle in his arms and held her close. "Promise me you won't try to get rid of me again. If there's a problem, let's talk about it, okay?"

"I promise."

CHAPTER TWENTY-NINE

OCTOBER 3

"Man, I'm starved!" David slid into the seat across from Michael.

"When aren't you hungry?"

"Hey, can I help it if I'm still growing?" David carried two hundred and fifty pounds on a muscular six foot, five inch frame. Since they were boys, David always ate more than anybody else as if he had a bottomless pit that constantly needed nourishment. In his defense, though, Michael had to admit that David was also very active. He played basketball twice a week and regularly worked out at the gym so maybe he was entitled to always be hungry. "What's going on, G? I haven't talked to you in a while. Mimi must be keeping you busy," David teased.

"We do spend a lot of time together," Michael agreed. "And if I have my way, we'll spend even more. I'm going to ask her to marry me."

"Marry?" David didn't realize their relationship was that serious, although Mimi was all Michael ever talked about. "Are you sure about this, G?"

"Positive. I've been in love with Michelle for a long time. When I met her the first time, I went home and told Dad that I met my wife. Then, as you know, we were separated for years. When I saw her again I knew that God was giving us another chance at love."

"Then I'm happy for you, man." David and Michael smacked high five. "What can I do?"

"Say you'll be my best man."

"That was already a given," David laughed. "If you ask anyone else, I'd hurt 'em." Michael didn't know whether he was joking or not.

"So when's the big event?"

"Soon, I hope."

"I'll have to let my folks know." Michael was like another son to Jason and Helen Watters and David knew his parents would be excited and happy for Michael. "You'll be the first of the musketeers to marry."

"Well, we don't know that for sure. Terrance might have been married for years now."

"True that," David agreed. "But since we don't know where he is, we'll assume you're the first."

"Okay."

"You know what that means don't you?" David prompted.

"I'm almost afraid to ask," Michael laughed.

"Dinner's on you!" David laughed. "No seriously man, I'm happy for you. I almost wish it were me."

"Come on David," Michael retorted. "Don't tell me you're ready to settle down."

"I've been ready for a while; I just can't convince a certain woman to take me seriously."

"So what is going on with you and Sarah?"

Before David could answer, he saw Miss Julia walking toward him. He slid out of the seat to stand just as she approached their table. When Michael saw who was coming, he also stood.

"David, it's good to see you again. It's been a while since you stopped in." Miss Julia offered her cheek for a kiss.

"Yes ma'am. I've been pretty busy at work and just grabbing stuff on the go." David ate at *Miss Julia's* at least twice a week because the food was so good and the portions were generous. "Do you remember Michael Stephens?"

"Of course," Julia replied as she turned toward Michael. "It's good to see you again. Is this your first time here?"

"Yes ma'am. David talks about the food all the time, but I have never had the opportunity to experience it until today."

"Everything's good. What did you order?"

"Crab cakes for me and ribs for David."

"Excellent choices. Make sure you save room for dessert. We have sweet potato pie and carrot cake."

"I'll have one of each." David had an uncontrollable sweet tooth.

"Good answer," Julia laughed. "I'm not going to keep you. I just wanted to stop by to say hello. Enjoy your meals." *Miss Julia's* was one of the more popular restaurants in Columbus because of the friendliness of the owner. She made it a point of coming out several times throughout the evening to speak to her customers. That, plus the excellent food and service kept the small establishment busy.

David watched Miss Julia as she walked away. "Man, if I want to know what Sarah's going to look like when she gets older, I only have to look at Miss Julia."

"They do look more like sisters than mother and daughter."

"I know."

"You never answered my question, David. What's going on with you and Sarah?"

"Man, I wish I knew." David was exasperated with the relationship, or non-relationship, which was more the case. Sarah knew that David was interested in her and had been for a while. She didn't mind hanging out with him as long as others were around, but whenever he remotely suggested a one-on-one date, she shut down. He tried talking to her about it without much success. The one time she did offer an excuse, she said it was because she was older than he was, as if eight years was that big of a deal. David shared his frustration with Michael.

"You're just going to have to hang in there, man. Some women just take longer than others to see the light, you know?"

"Yeah, I know," David muttered. "But why can't we be like you and Mimi? You know, love at first sight?"

"Be careful what you wish for, bro," Michael cautioned. "Don't forget, we were separated for twelve long years. And trying to stay positive and upbeat was a real challenge." Michael paused while the server brought their food. He waited until she left before continuing, "The only thing that kept me going was my belief that we would get together again. It was a faith walk that paid off."

"It sure did."

"Sometimes it just takes a minute for couples to click," Michael continued. "Dad said that my mom wasn't interested in giving him the time of day when they first met, and even Pastor Hooper said that Lady

Hooper couldn't stand him at first. So don't give up on Sarah yet," Michael encouraged.

"I know you're talking right, G. It's just hard to handle a broken heart," David acknowledged. "I've been accused of breaking women's hearts before, but it's never happened to me. I don't like it!"

"I hear you, man. But if God doesn't bring you two together, you wouldn't want the relationship anyway, right?"

"Right. I just pray that God wants us to be together," David confessed. "Sarah is my best female friend and I love her. I could spend the rest of my life with her by my side. I can even see a bunch of little Watters running around. I think she's afraid of being hurt, but I would never do that to her."

"She knows that, man."

"I know she knows it in her head," David agreed. "I just need her to get it in her heart."

"Yeah, but what are you going to do?"

"If I had the answer to that, we would be together by now."

"I hear that. But, hey, look on the bright side. When Michelle agrees to marry me, you know she'll probably ask Sarah to be in the wedding. And you're in the wedding. Which means the two of you will have to spend time together rehearsing and stuff."

David hadn't thought of that possibility and perked up. This could work. Maybe he would have a chance to talk to Sarah again. He just needed to know what the problem was, because he didn't really believe it had anything to do with their ages. There had to be something more and he was determined to find out exactly what it was. "Yeah," David began eating with gusto. "That's a good plan."

CHAPTER THIRTY

OCTOBER 12
CLEVELAND, OHIO

Donavon unlocked the screen door and let Michael in. "Hi, son. What brings you to Cleveland so early in the morning?"

Michael glanced at his watch and saw that it was only six thirty. He was glad his father was an early riser. "Sorry Dad. I couldn't sleep and just started driving."

"What's the matter Michael?" Donavon took a mug from the cabinet and poured Michael a cup of coffee.

"I'm going to ask Michelle to marry me tonight."

"Congratulations son, that's great." Donavon put the mug down and grabbed Michael in a bear hug. "Michelle's a nice girl. I like her."

"She likes you, too. And Brianna, Calvin and the kids. I just don't know how she feels about me," Michael admitted.

"Have you asked her?"

"Well, no. But I'm pretty sure she loves me. I know I love her. We've been together since May. I think I'm just nervous."

"Probably. And that's a good sign. The last thing you want is to come across as arrogant and assume that she has to say yes. On the other hand, after spending so much time together, you should have a feel for where she is. Have you told her it was you and David who found her that day?"

Michael had called his father the night after Michelle explained about being raped. He had no choice but to acknowledge that she was the one that he and David had found that day so long ago. His father and David encouraged him to tell her as soon as possible so there wouldn't be anything between them, but Michael was reluctant. He didn't know how she was going to respond and he didn't want to take a chance that she would be too embarrassed to continue seeing him.

"Not yet," Michael responded. "I'm going to tell her tonight. I'll ask her to marry me first and then I'll tell her about finding her that day."

"Hmm. Have you thought about how you'll pop the question?"

"Michelle's coming over for dinner tonight. I'll feed her and then ask her to marry me."

"Sounds like a good plan. Do you already have a ring?"

"Yes sir. I went to see Uncle Jerry the day after I saw Michelle again. He sold me the perfect ring. Let me show you." Michael reached into his jeans pocket.

"You brought it with you?"

"I've carried it with me every day since I got it," Michael chuckled. "I want to be ready whenever the moment strikes. Is that silly, Dad?"

"No son. You're in love. You're allowed to do silly things. Let's look at that ring."

Michael opened the deep green velvet case and extended it to his father. "This looks to be about two and a half carats, flawless, good clarity. Marquis center stone, baguette accents, platinum setting. This is an excellent cut and workmanship. Jeremiah designed this himself, didn't he?" Donavon concluded.

"Yes sir. Look at you, sounding like an expert," Michael teased.

"I should be. After being friends with Jerry for over fifty years, he would be insulted if I hadn't picked up anything about the business. I could always get my jeweler's loupe," Donavon offered.

"That's okay, Dad." Michael knew his father didn't have a jeweler's loupe and was just teasing. He was also aware that his father had picked up quite of bit of knowledge from Uncle Jerry over the years and knew what he was talking about.

"I know he gave you a good price, didn't he?"

"Uncle Jerry sold me the ring and matching band for five thousand. I figured it was his way of honoring your friendship, right?"

"I'm sure. That's an excellent price." Donavon knew the ring alone was at least twenty-five thousand dollars retail. "I would do the same for Terrance and Jeremiah knows it."

Michael and Donavon were silent as they thought of Terrance. He had been such an integral part of their earlier lives so it seemed appropriate to have a moment of silence. "Do you think we'll ever see him again Dad?"

"I don't know. Jerry hasn't heard from him in a long time, but a father would never forget his son. I pray that he's okay and we'll see him again soon."

"David and I talk about him every now and then. He just disappeared overnight."

"It's sad all right. Maybe one day we'll find out what happened. In the meantime, you need to get going so you can prepare for your big night."

"You're right. I still need to go shopping and there's a restaurant Michelle likes in Mansfield that makes great lemon meringue pies. That's her favorite."

"And here I thought you came to see me," Donavon said laughing.

Michael joined his father in laughter. "I did, Dad. But why not use everything to my advantage?" Michael took two apples from the fruit bowl and headed for the back door. "Thanks, Dad."

"You're welcome, son. I'm very proud of you. If Mom were alive, she'd be proud of you, too. Michelle's a great girl. Looks like both my children have found true love and I couldn't be happier. Drive safe and know that I'm praying for you."

CHAPTER THIRTY-ONE

"**Y**ou made it." Michael leaned down to kiss Michelle.

"Finally." Michelle returned the kiss.

"I've missed you," Michael said. "How did the presentation go?"

"I think we'll get the account," Michelle confidently responded. She had been working for the past two weeks on a proposal for a large firm. Consequently, she and Michael hadn't spent as much time together as they would like, but getting this account would be a big boost for her business.

"Way to go! I knew you could do it. I'm proud of you, baby."

"Thanks. Something smells very good."

"Just follow your nose. Everything's ready." Michael led her to the dining room.

"The table looks nice," Michelle said as Michael seated her. The table was set with fresh flowers, candles and crystal.

"Thanks. We aim to please at *Chez Michael's*."

"So how was your day?"

"It was busy and very productive. I went to Cleveland to see Dad and picked up lemon meringue pie for you." He couldn't tell her that he was on the road early that morning because then he would have to explain why he couldn't sleep. He wanted the proposal to be a surprise.

"That's so sweet of you." Michael spoiled her with his thoughtfulness. "So how is your father?"

"He's fine and sends you his love."

"He's a nice man."

"Yeah, he's cool. When does your project start?"

"Not until the first part of January."

"So what are you going to do until then?"

"There's always something that needs to be done, but I'm going to spend some time just doing nothing." Michelle smiled impishly at Michael. "I'll think of you while I'm relaxing."

"I just bet you will."

"This is delicious." Michael had prepared beef stroganoff, a mesclun green salad with a walnut vinaigrette dressing and sourdough rolls. "You're so talented. I just might have to keep you around," Michelle joked.

"I hope so."

Finishing the last of his dinner, Michael asked about dessert.

"Are you kidding?" Michelle responded. "I'm stuffed. I might not even have room for my nightly ice cream."

"Oh, no! Not the ice cream."

"Yes, the ice cream! And it's your fault. The stroganoff was wonderful. Do I get to take home a care package?"

"Sure. I'm glad you liked it." Michael walked around the table and offered Michelle his hand. "Let's go to the living room."

"Let me help with the dishes."

"No. You just relax for a few minutes." Michael kissed her briefly on the lips. "I won't be long." He cleared the table, loaded the dishwasher and then discovered Michelle dozing on the couch when he went into the living room. He loaded the CD player with their favorite jazz artists, dimmed the lights and lit candles throughout the room. Satisfied with his efforts, Michael knelt down beside the couch. He gently stroked Michelle's cheek until she woke up.

"I am so sorry, Michael. Did I fall asleep?"

"Uh-huh."

"Was I asleep for very long?"

"Not long. You must have been tired."

Michelle nodded her head. "I didn't snore did I? That would be too embarrassing!"

"No, you didn't snore. Are you feeling better?"

"Actually I am."

"Good. There's something I want to talk to you about."

"Sounds ominous."

"No, not that bad. But it is serious."

"Okay."

"Do you remember the very first day we met?"

"Of course."

"I want to read you what I wrote in my journal that day." Michael pulled a folded piece of paper out of his pocket and read:

Dear God. Today I met my wife. I always knew you had someone special for me. I just didn't realize that I was going to meet her today. It's her birthday and I received the gift. Thank you, God. I hope I made a good impression on her. She is so pretty and funny and smart and nice. I want to spend the rest of my life with her. Thanks God for sending her my way.

Michael re-folded the paper and put it on the end table. He took Michelle's hand and continued talking. "I wrote that not knowing that we wouldn't see each other for twelve years. I always believed I would see you again. I didn't know when, how or even where, but I knew that God would answer my prayer. When you opened the door a few months ago, my heart felt like it was going to pop out of my chest. All I could think about was the second chance He was giving me with you.

"When we went out on our first "official" date and I told you I hadn't met the right woman, that wasn't true. I had met her and she was sitting across from me eating peach ice cream. I couldn't tell you then because I didn't want to scare you off. I didn't want you to think I was some kind of nut telling you that God said you were to be my wife, although I knew you were the one. I love you and I want to spend the rest of my life making you happy. How do you feel about me?"

"I love you, too," Michelle tearfully responded.

"Whew! That's a relief. There's something else I have to tell you." Michael sat on the couch and put his arm around Michelle. He mentally discarded his plan to ask her to marry him first. He needed to clear the air. "Do you remember the night you told me about the rape and how two boys found you and took you to the hospital?"

"Umm." Michelle loved the smell of Michael's cologne and was still giddy from him saying he loved her. Had she really heard him mention marriage?

"That was me and David."

"What?" She tried to straighten up, but Michael tightened his arm around her. "Hear me out. David made the connection the night we were re-introduced, but it took me longer. I didn't figure it out until the night you told me about the rape..."

"Oh. My. God."

"...and I've been trying to find a way to tell you about it since that night."

"You saved my life. Everybody said so." Michelle broke from Michael's embrace so she could look him in the eye. "It was you who carried me to the hospital, wasn't it?"

"Yes," Michael confessed. "I was so scared. David and I had been fooling around in the park and took a shortcut to one of our friend's house. We heard you moaning before we saw you."

"I'm so glad you did. How can I ever thank you and David?"

"Baby, you don't owe me any thanks. We did what I hope anyone would have done. I prayed for you so hard that day and the next. David told me your mom called to thank us."

"My mom?"

"Yeah. She got David's name and phone number from one of the officers who knew his father."

"She never told me, but that sounds like her."

"David said she was real nice."

"She was. I wish you could have known her."

"I do, too. Now that you know the secret I've been carrying around for a few weeks," Michael paused briefly, "Sienna Michelle Nickelson, will you marry me?"

"Yes!" Michelle flung her arms around Michael's neck and squeezed. "Yes!"

"Hallelujah!" Michael removed the ring case from his pocket. "Will you accept this as a token of my affection?"

Michelle opened the box and gasped. "Oh, Michael," Michelle breathed. "I've never seen anything like this. It's positively beautiful."

"This is a beautiful ring for a beautiful woman. I hope it fits."

"I'm sure it will."

Michael slipped the ring on her finger and smiled when they realized it was a perfect fit. Michael softly brushed his mustache across her fingers. "The day after I came to your house with David, I called one of my Cleveland clients, Uncle Jerry, who owns a jewelry store..."

"Are you talking about Mr. Jeremiah?"

"Yes and..."

"Of Sanctuary Jewelers?"

"Yeah, see..."

"He's your uncle?"

"Not really. See..."

"But he's one of your clients?" Michelle couldn't stop interrupting. She shouldn't be nervous. He had already popped the question.

"Yes. He and my father have been friends since childhood. When I started my company Uncle Jerry left Stewardson and Smythe and came with me."

"I love his jewelry." Sanctuary Jewelers was one of the most exclusive jewelry stores in the Cleveland area.

"Good. Now can I finish my story about the ring?"

"Oh, I'm sorry. Please continue."

"Anyway, I called Uncle Jerry and told him I had found my wife and needed the best he had. We scheduled an appointment and when I got to the store, he took me to the back room and showed me this ring. He created it about thirteen years ago and kept it in the vault all this time. He didn't know who it was for, but believed that God would send the right person for it. After I called him, he said God told him the ring was for me.

"Every time that we've been together I've had this with me, waiting for the right moment. God revealed to me that tonight was the night to ask you. I promise to spend the rest of my life devoted to you. I love you," Michael finished as he bent to kiss Michelle. "So, when can we get married?"

"Michael! I haven't had time to think about it."

"I have. Let's get married next month," Michael suggested.

"I can't get married in a month!" Michelle protested.

"Sure you can. I don't want to wait any longer for you to become my wife."

"There's too much to do. I don't have a dress..."

"I'll help you. Do you want a large wedding?"

"No. I've always dreamed of a small intimate wedding."

"Sounds perfect. I like the idea of a small wedding. And we can pull that off in a month, can't we?"

"I guess we could." Michelle didn't want to wait either. "Okay, let's get married next month!"

CHAPTER THIRTY-TWO

OCTOBER 21

Michelle was pleased to see quite a few items already checked off on her "Operation Wedding Day" list. They had gotten a lot accomplished in two weeks. True to his word, Michael had helped. A friend of his owned a printing company and he expedited the wedding invitations. Fortunately, the list was small and they were able to get the invitations printed and in the mail within a week.

David's mom, Helen, told Michelle about a small boutique outside of Cleveland that might have what she was looking for in a wedding dress. She wasn't sure what type of dress she wanted, but she knew she would recognize it when she saw it. Sure enough she found the perfect one: a champagne colored, tea length, long sleeve designer gown. Michelle discovered that she already had shoes the exact same color.

Michelle asked Sarah, Maria and Stephanie to be her maids of honor; Brianna would be her matron of honor. David and Calvin were going to stand with Michael, as well as two of his cousins. Uncle Carl was going to give Michelle away.

Miss Julia agreed to cater the reception, and one of Michael's clients offered them the use of his luxurious home for the reception site. He was going to be out of the country and wanted that to be his wedding gift. The client did a lot of entertaining so the house was already equipped with a fully functional gourmet kitchen and could easily hold fifty people.

They solved the problem of where to live by deciding to rent Michelle's condo and live in Michael's house. Michelle knew she was going to love her new home, especially the master suite. The bathroom was oversized and equipped with a Jacuzzi, glass shower for two, dual sinks and a water closet. The bedroom had two very large walk-in closets and a see-through fireplace that adjoined the sitting room on the other side of a half wall. Just off the sitting room was a kitchenette. The rest of the house included three bedrooms, two and a half bathrooms, a great room, a gourmet kitchen, formal dining room, a home theater and an office slash conference area equipped with a drop down screen.

We just might be able to pull this off, Michelle thought as she went to the kitchen to start dinner. She had just taken a chicken and rice casserole out of the freezer when the phone rang. "Hello."

"Is it true?"

"Excuse me?" Michelle didn't recognize the male caller's voice.

"Is it true?"

"Who is this?"

"Is. It. True? Are you really getting married?"

Recognition finally dawned and Michelle sighed. "Amari?"

"Yeah. Are you really getting married?"

"Why would you care? We haven't spoken to each other in over five years. Who do you think you are calling me?"

"Just because I haven't talked to you doesn't mean I haven't thought about you."

"Yeah, right. Tell me another one."

"It's true, Mimi. I have thought about you and I've asked Nikki about you. She said you were more into the Jesus thing than ever so I didn't call."

"Is that how you found out I'm getting married?"

"So it is true?"

"Yes, Amari. I'm getting married in two weeks."

"Well, to answer your question, I saw the announcement in the paper."

"So why call me now?"

"Who is this man? What do you know about him?"

"Whoa! Don't try to act like you're jealous. We may have kicked it back in the day, but we didn't have a mad, passionate affair so don't act like you're wounded. It was just sex. And just for the record, you gave up the right to question me about my business a long time ago. So cut the crap Amari. Why are you calling me now?"

"I don't want to see you make a mistake."

"What are you talking about? You don't even know Michael."

"Nikki told me about him."

"And?"

"And he sounds like a nerd," Amari smugly concluded.

"Nerd? Michael may be a lot of things, but he's certainly not a nerd. He's handsome, intelligent, kind, owns his own business; he has financial stability…

"Yeah, yeah, yeah. But does he do for you what I can?"

"You mean what you did, not can. What we had is over."

"Don't be so sure about that, sweet thing."

"Oh, I'm sure. And don't call me sweet thing!"

"Nikki said he's a church boy."

"He's not a boy. He's a man, and Nikki talks too much."

"How else would I know what's going on with you?"

"You haven't cared for a while. And since when did you and Nikki become such bosom buddies?"

"Are you jealous?"

"In your dreams," Michelle snorted.

"Don't worry. She's not my type, you are."

"This conversation is over and don't call me again!"

"Before you hang up, let me just say one more thing."

"What?"

"When Nerd Boy can't satisfy your itch, give me a call. I haven't forgotten what you like and how you like it."

Michelle slammed the phone shut. Who did he think he was talking to her like that? And what was Nikki's problem? Before Michelle could think about it, she dialed Nikki's cell phone.

"Hi, Mimi. How are the wedding plans coming along?"

"I just got off the phone with Amari. Have you been talking to him about me?"

"I ran into him at a book store last week. Why?"

Michelle relayed the conversation with Amari and was still fuming that he had the gall to call.

"Mimi, I am so sorry. Amari seemed so sincere when he asked how you were doing. When he asked if you were seeing anyone, I told him that you were engaged to be married. He wanted to know who you were marrying and I told him about Michael. I never said anything negative about him. If I thought for one minute he would have called you, I would never have said anything to him. Please forgive me."

"It's okay. I just wasn't expecting to hear from him. He's so arrogant and when he called Michael 'Nerd Boy,' I could have reached through the phone and smacked him."

"Nerd Boy? There's nothing nerdy about Michael. Amari's just trying to get under your skin."

"I know. He succeeded, which is why I hung up on him. Do me a favor and don't say anything else about me."

"Don't worry. I've learned my lesson, believe me."

Michelle almost felt sorry for Amari, because she knew the next time Nikki saw him she was going to set him straight. It didn't matter that he was almost a foot taller than she was. If Nikki had to stand on a chair to get in his face, Michelle knew that Amari was in for a good tongue lashing. She almost wished she could see it.

CHAPTER THIRTY-THREE

NOVEMBER 8

"**W**hen will Michael be back?" Aunt Shirley asked. She and her husband, Carl, had come to Columbus earlier in the week and were staying with Michelle.

"He'll be back early tomorrow morning and then he's off until after the honeymoon."

"Umm, the honeymoon," Shirley teased. "Are you getting excited?"

"I'm excited. I'm nervous. I'm scared," Michelle confessed.

"Marriage is a big step all right," Shirley agreed. "But when you find the one God has for you, it makes all the difference in the world. Keeping God first will help you over a lot of hurdles." She should know, Michelle thought. She'd been married to Carl Nickelson for fifty-two years.

"What kind of hurdles?"

"Well, the usual. Trying to make the adjustment of living with another person, discovering likes and dislikes, that sort of thing. Just don't let molehills become mountains and you'll do fine. Michael's a good man and he loves the Lord. That's important."

"I know Aunt Shirley. It's one of the things I admire about him. He's a mighty man of faith."

"And you're a mighty woman of faith. I was worried about you a few years ago. You were heading in the wrong direction, but God helped you to turn your life around. You've come a long way, honey, and I'm proud of you. I wish Betty were still alive. She'd be busting a gut."

"I wish your father could be here," Carl interjected. He was finishing up the last of his lasagna while listening to the women talk.

"Why?" Michelle snorted. "Even if he were still alive, he probably wouldn't have come to the wedding."

"What are you talking about?"

"My father hated me and you know it."

"I know of no such thing," Carl said. "And neither do you."

"Yes, you do," Michelle insisted. "You saw how he treated me and..."

"Wait one minute, young lady. You might be getting married in a few days, but you're still not old enough to sass me. Your father loved you the best he knew how."

"If you say so, but I was there, remember? I know the mean things he did and said every chance he got, and there's no way that can be equated to love. I apologize for being disrespectful Uncle Carl, but you didn't have to live with Dad."

"Mimi, you're going to have to trust me on this one. My brother loved you and your mother more than you'll ever know."

"Do you know why he hated me?"

"He didn't hate you!"

"Okay, do you know why he wasn't able to show love and affection the way most people do?" she sarcastically asked.

"Watch your mouth, girl," Carl cautioned.

"Do you, Uncle Carl? Aunt Shirley? Why did Dad make my life so miserable? It wasn't always that way. I remember laughing and playing with Dad when I was little. What made him change?" The look Carl and Shirley exchanged was uneasy and made Michelle all the more determined to find out what they were hiding. There had to be a reason why her father turned against her and she knew it had nothing to do with anything she had done. "Do you know something about him I don't?"

Neither Shirley nor Carl answered Michelle right away. Finally, Carl cleared his throat. "That's a grown-up question little girl. Are you sure you're ready for a grown-up answer?"

"I'm ready for whatever you have to say that will explain why a man who was supposed to look out for me, love me and take care of me treated me like the scum of the earth."

Carl nodded his head and knew that the time had come for Mimi to be told the truth about her father. He had tried talking to Donald about his behavior, but the conversations always ended up in shouting matches, more on Donald's part than Carl's. Donald refused to see that what he was doing was creating a wedge that would be hard to get around. Betty died without receiving Donald's forgiveness for something he thought she had done, and Michelle had grown into a physically beautiful woman with internal scars from her father's emotional abuse. Carl often thought it would have been better if Donald had just physically left his family instead of staying in the house and withdrawing emotionally. "Your father thought your mother had an affair and that you weren't his child," Carl mumbled.

"What?" Michelle whispered.

"He thought your mother had an affair and that you weren't his child," Carl repeated louder. He had held the secret long enough. Michelle was old enough to handle the truth.

"When your parents first married, they tried for several years to have a child and couldn't. Your mother was tested by the doctor, but he couldn't find any reason why she couldn't get pregnant. Donald assumed that since Betty had been tested the fault had to be his, but he was too stubborn to find out for sure.

"Donald was under a lot of pressure in those early days. Your mother was very beautiful and Donald never understood how someone who looked like her could want him. The first time he asked her out, he thought she was joking when she said yes. But your mother saw something in Donald that convinced her to take a chance on him. Donald never felt worthy and wouldn't believe Betty's affirmations of love."

"Wait a minute, Uncle Carl. Why would he think he wasn't good enough?"

"He thought he was ugly."

"How could he think that? Why would he think that?"

"Because our mother told him he was."

"What?"

"You never had the chance to know your paternal grandparents. Your grandfather, my father, left when I was fifteen and your father was five. Mother couldn't handle it and started drinking. When she was drunk she would start screaming and hitting Donald. I intervened as much as I could, but there was only so much I could do. As far as Mother was concerned, Donald was a mistake. She thought she was finished having babies and ten years after having me she found herself pregnant again. That's partly why Dad left. He couldn't handle the responsibility and took the easy way out."

"Is my grandfather still alive?"

"No. He got into a bar fight and lost. That really sent Mother over the edge and she snapped. I guess she kept hoping he would come back and they would get back together. I really don't know. Anyway, for most of Donald's life, he heard Mother call him stupid, ugly, no account and so on. After a while I guess it became part of him."

"But why would his mother do that?"

"Because he looked just like Dad. I guess she figured if she couldn't get to Dad, she would do the next best thing and take it out on Donald."

"So how did he meet Mom?"

"I introduced them," Shirley interjected.

"I never knew that!"

"Your mom and I met through a mutual friend and just hit it off, even though she was a lot younger. When Donald came home from the service, he wasn't seeing anyone special and I told Betty about Donald. She was willing to meet him so we went on a double date. One thing led to another and they started dating."

"But," Carl picked up the story, "Donald just couldn't get it through his head that Betty really cared for him."

"But he obviously asked her to marry him."

"I didn't say it made sense. I think deep down Donald wanted to believe that Betty really loved him, but he couldn't make his head and his heart agree. He always felt that the first chance she got she would leave him so he became possessive. If a man glanced her way, Donald made a big production out of it. One day he saw the mailman talking to Betty and went crazy when he heard her laughing. He yelled, cursed and screamed at her like he had lost his mind. He actually drew back his fist to hit her, but something stopped him. That was all Betty needed. She left him and moved in with one of her girlfriends for almost six months.

"During their separation, Donald repeatedly apologized and promised never to do anything like that again. Betty finally accepted his apology and moved back into the house. When they reconciled, by some miracle, she became pregnant. Donald and Betty were so happy. I wish you could have known them both back then. It was like they were newlyweds all over again. They planned and saved for your arrival. I helped him paint the bedroom yellow and Shirley helped Betty make curtains, pillows and toys for your room. It really was an exciting time for all of us. My brother seemed to have gotten rid of the demons chasing him and Betty was smiling again.

"The day you were born, I thought you would go blind from all the flash bulbs," Carl laughed. "Your father bought so much film and took so many pictures that the nurses finally told him to stop. He didn't care. He had a child, a daughter, and he couldn't have been prouder. Betty teased him about how you would wrap him around your finger and he boasted about all the things he would teach you.

"You looked just like your mother. You had her mannerisms, her looks and even her temperament. You were a good baby and a good little girl. Everyone who saw you and Betty together said you two looked like twins. It didn't bother Donald that physically you didn't seem to have anything from our side of the family.

"Everything was fine until your father got laid off from work. You would have been about six or seven at that time. There was hardly any work to be found, but your father took whatever jobs he could to keep a roof over you and Betty's head and food on the table. He had lined up a construction job that paid pretty good money, but it took him out of town more than he liked. Donald did what he had to do. When the job was finished, the men were given a bonus for bringing it in on time. Donald decided to stop for a beer on his way home. There was a man bragging about all the women he had over the years and described in great detail everything he and these women did together. Some of the men were egging him on and he was happy to keep talking as long as they kept buying the beer.

"He described one woman who was the spitting image of your mother, and your father went ballistic. He went home and accused Betty of having an affair. No matter how much she denied it, Donald never forgave her for what he believed was a major transgression. Unfortunately, he took it out on you. It was my mother all over again. I tried

120

talking to him once and he confessed that every time he looked at you, he was reminded of what Betty had done. He knew that the way he was treating you wasn't right, but he couldn't seem to stop."

"Did she have an affair?" Michelle knew she had to ask the question even if she wasn't going to like the answer.

"I don't believe she did. But there was no convincing Donald. The only thing he based it on was a drunk's description of a woman. He had no other proof."

"And because of that he made my life miserable?" The more Michelle thought about it, the more upset she became. "This is unbelievable! He wasted all the years we could have had together because of something he thought happened. Why didn't he believe Mom?"

"There are probably a lot of reasons, but I think the main one is that he just couldn't believe that a beautiful woman would love him."

"I can't believe this! Are you sure that's the only reason?" It just didn't make sense that her father would turn on her because of something he thought had happened. Why wouldn't he have tried to find proof of an affair instead of taking the word of a stranger? All those years wasted. Without warning Michelle burst into tears. Shirley took her in her arms and held her while she cried. When Michelle's tears finally subsided, Carl reached for her hand.

"There is another reason why your father acted the way he did," Carl confessed. He had come this far. Michelle needed to hear the whole story. "He felt guilty."

"Why?" Michelle wasn't sure she could take anything else, but she had to know.

"He had an affair."

"What? When?" Michelle jerked her hand from Carl's and angrily stood up. How dare he accuse her mother of doing the very thing he had done? No wonder he couldn't look at her without feeling guilty. It was probably like a knife in the back every time he saw his child who was the spitting image of his wife whom he had cheated on.

"It was during the time of their separation. I think part of the problem was that because Donald had cheated, he assumed Betty had, too. When the man in the bar started talking, he jumped on that as a way of not having to deal with what he had done."

121

"Did Mom ever know?"

"I don't think so. And I believe it only happened during the time of their separation. In his own way, Donald loved both you and your mother. He just didn't know how to properly show it."

"Yeah, right."

"He was my brother and I'm not condoning what he did. I gave him heck when he finally confessed everything to me. But it was in the past and he assured me it was only that one time. I'm sorry for the way he treated you. I tried my best to get him to see that he was making a big mistake, but the guilt was too much for him to get around."

"I'm sorry, too."

"Are you okay, honey?" Aunt Shirley asked.

"My head hurts."

"Why don't you go lie down? I'll put the food away."

"You don't mind, Aunt Shirley?"

"No, honey, I don't mind. You go take care of yourself and we'll see you in the morning."

Michelle kissed her aunt's cheek, "Thanks Aunt Shirley. Good-night Uncle Carl."

"Goodnight, baby. I know you've got a lot to think about, but just remember God will help you process everything if you just turn it over to him."

CHAPTER THIRTY-FOUR

NOVEMBER 12

Michelle woke with a smile on her face. "Thank you God," she whispered. "I can't believe my wedding day is finally here." A lot has happened in the last month and once again God demonstrated His control over time and events. When Michael proposed and said he wanted to get married in a month, it didn't seem like thirty days would be enough. Then it seemed like the month wouldn't end and her wedding day would ever arrive. Finally it was here—the beginning of a postcard-perfect fall day when she would become Michael's wife. Michelle giggled and threw the covers back just as a knock sounded on the door. "Come in," she sang out.

"Good morning, honey," Shirley entered with a tray weighed down with waffles, bacon, juice and coffee. "I thought you would enjoy breakfast in bed before you get going. We have a busy day ahead of us." Carl had arranged for Shirley, Michelle, Sarah, Maria, Stephanie, Brianna and her daughter, Amanda, to go to an upscale salon for a full day of pampering before the wedding. A limousine would drop them off and return at five o'clock to get them to the church in time for the six o'clock candlelight service.

"Thanks Aunt Shirley, this smells wonderful, but I don't know if I can eat."

"You have to eat something or you'll make yourself sick. It's a long time until the reception."

"Yes ma'am."

"Are you all packed?"

"Just about. I want to add a few of the gifts from yesterday and then I'll be finished." Sarah and Brianna had hosted a personal bridal shower the day before and her friends went all out with the lingerie, teddies and camisoles. She had never seen so much lace and silk in her life, but her absolute favorite gift was a chocolate and gold peignoir set that her friend Mother Henderson had given her. She wanted Michelle's wedding to start off right and told her that in the sixty-six years she was married to her late husband, Wilbur, he never saw her sleep in anything flannel or cotton.

"The shower was nice wasn't it?" Shirley was saying. "I hadn't seen Stephanie and Maria since we moved to Florida, but you three used to be real close. Do you still keep in touch?"

"I see Maria all the time since she's just in Cleveland. I haven't seen Stephanie in almost a year, but we e-mail each other every week." Maria taught first grade and was married to Peter who ran his family's plumbing business. Stephanie married her high-school boyfriend, Darryl, a dentist, moved to San Diego and had two sets of the cutest twin boys you would ever want to see.

"It's good that you've stayed friends all these years. Friendships are important."

"Amen, Aunt Shirley."

"I have something to give you," Shirley handed Michelle a tissue-wrapped package.

"Oh, Aunt Shirley. You and Uncle Carl have already done so much. I don't need anything else."

"This is something that belongs to you anyway."

Michelle opened the tissue and discovered a photograph of her mother taken the year before she died. "Where in the world did you find this?" Michelle's eyes dampened as she looked at the photo.

"I was looking through an old album and this was stuck in between some loose pictures. I knew you would want to have it."

"Thanks Aunt Shirley."

"If your mother were alive, she would be sitting here instead of me."

"I miss her so much. Even after all these years."

"Death doesn't stop love's memories."

"I believe that. I just wish she were here."

"I know you do honey, but you know she's always in your heart."

"Okay, let's change the subject before I really start crying," Michelle sniffled.

"Before the day's over you will have cried, laughed and cried some more. Weddings bring out all of your emotions."

"Aunt Shirley, do you remember your wedding day?"

"Of course, child," Shirley smiled in response. "A woman never forgets one of the most important days of her life. I can remember it like it was yesterday. It was a very cold, snowy day in January but we didn't care. My parents didn't have a lot of money, but they made it as nice as they could. Everything was beautiful."

"That sounds nice."

"It was. I'm not going to tell you that every day has been smooth. But I will tell you that if you make the commitment to work things out, you will enjoy the adventure of being married."

"Adventure?"

"Oh, yes. A wedding is an event, but marriage is an adventure. If you think of it that way then nothing that happens will surprise you and you won't let little things work your nerves, including trying to figure out why he can't remember to put the toilet seat down."

"Aunt Shirley, you're priceless!"

"That's why I've been married over fifty years and some couples can't make it fifty days," Shirley laughed.

CHAPTER THIRTY-FIVE

Six hours later the ladies were waiting for the ceremony to begin. They had been buffed, polished, waxed, coifed and perfumed and were anxious for their efforts to be appreciated. They looked good, smelled good and felt good.

Sarah responded to the soft tap on the door because she was closest. It took all of her strength not to do an impersonation of the wicked witch melting at the end of *The Wizard of Oz* movie when she saw who was standing on the other side. It should be against the law for any man to look this good, Sarah thought. At six feet five inches, two hundred and fifty pounds, David Watters had both the height and physique to compliment a custom-made tuxedo. Sarah schooled her features to hide her response. "Hi."

David's eyes traveled the length of Sarah from the top of her short curly hair to the crimson colored satin shoes on her feet and everything in between. "Sarah," he whispered, "You look beautiful!"

"Thank you, David." They allowed their eyes to share all the things they couldn't, or wouldn't, say out loud. David's plans to talk to Sarah during the rehearsal didn't go quite right since she was never alone. He didn't know if he would get a chance to talk to her this evening either even though he was escorting her up and down the aisle. Now here she was looking so pretty it took his breath away.

"Who's at the door," Brianna asked as she looked around Sarah. "Oh, it's just you. Hi, David." Brianna saw the stupefied look on David's face and recognized it immediately. She had seen the same look on Calvin's face when he was finally ready to get serious about her. She had seen the way David would sneak looks at Sarah when he thought no one was watching and smiled to herself. Unless she was badly mistaken, Sarah's single days were numbered and it couldn't happen to a nicer couple. "Why are you here?" Brianna asked. David kept looking at Sarah without responding.

"Earth to David," Brianna teased.

"Huh?"

"Why are you here?" she asked again.

David reluctantly tore his gaze away from Sarah and looked at Brianna. "Oh, uh, Michael wanted me to give this to Michelle." David handed her a flat oblong-shaped box.

"Okay, I'll make sure she gets it. Was there anything else you needed?"

"Uh, no, that was it."

"Okay, we'll see you in a few minutes," Brianna said and gently closed the door and patted Sarah on the shoulder. "It's okay. We've all been there."

Sarah laid her head against the door and closed her eyes. What had just happened? *I've never had a reaction like that to David before. I've always been able to keep my feelings hidden so why today of all days would my emotions go haywire. Why now? Why today?*

"Who was at the door?" Michelle asked.

"David. He had a gift from Michael." Brianna handed the box to Michelle who pulled the ribbon and discovered a hand-written letter:

> *My dearest Michelle. I fell in love with you the first moment I saw you all those years ago and I knew we were destined to be together. That afternoon sitting in the food court eating ice cream I fell in love with your spirit as well as your physical beauty.*
>
> *While we were away from each other, a piece of my heart stopped beating because it belonged to you. But I knew that one day, some how, some where, some way, we would be together again. I promised myself that when that happened we would never be separated again.*
>
> *I've waited my entire adult life for you and to-day God will answer my prayer and allow us to be-come one. In a very few moments Pastor Hooper will*

say the words that legally makes us man and wife. We will become one spiritually before the eyes of God, our family and friends. A few hours later we will become one physically, and I'll be allowed to give free reign to my passion. The poet asked, "How do I love thee?" I can't answer that question yet because time has not revealed all of the wonderful things you are. I can, however, tell you that I vow to spend the rest of my life discovering the many facets of you.

I want to know what you look like in the morning with the sun beaming on your face. I want to know what you look like with your hair spread over the pillow with the moonlight as your only covering. I want to create sweet, precious memories with you. I want to spend all the rest of my appointed days with you by my side.

You are the symphony of my soul, and I love you.

Michelle read the letter twice and knew the words came straight from Michael's heart because they went directly to hers. With tears streaming down her face she turned to her friends. "Michael wrote me a love letter," she whispered. The women looked at each and smiled.

CHAPTER THIRTY-SIX

One month to the day she was asked and two Saturdays before Thanksgiving, Sienna Michelle Nickelson became Mrs. Gregory Michael Stephens in front of fifty friends and family members at the Christian Center. After the ceremony they traveled en masse to the reception where Miss Julia had created a buffet with enough food to feed an army.

About an hour later, Donavon saw Sarah approaching him with the caterer whom he assumed was her older sister.

"Hi Mr. Stephens," Sarah said as she hugged Michael's father. "This is my mother."

"This can't be your mother."

"Julia Caldwell, Donavon Stephens," Sarah performed the introductions.

"It's nice to meet you, Mr. Stephens," Julia said while extending her hand. "I've heard a lot about you."

"Donavon. It's nice to meet you, too, Ms. Caldwell." Donavon couldn't get over how much they looked alike.

"Julia, please."

"Julia. You two look like sisters, not mother and daughter." Julia and Sarah exchanged smiles. They had come to expect that reaction whenever people saw them together. After all, there was only thirteen years difference between them, but Donavon didn't need to know that.

"Thank you. We hear that often."

"Am I to understand that you catered this delicious food?"

"Yes, I own *Miss Julia's* on Sinclair Boulevard. You'll have to stop in one night as my guest."

"I'll make sure to do that. If this food is any indication of your skill, you must have a loyal following."

"Yes, we do."

Donavon and Julia stood smiling at one another and Sarah realized she had been forgotten. Hmm, what's going on here? "Mommy, I'm going to go check on something, okay."

"Sure honey."

"I'll be right back, okay?"

"Don't worry about your mother," Donavon said, "I'll make sure she's taken care of."

CHAPTER THIRTY-SEVEN

"**G**irl, the ceremony was beautiful and your dress is gorgeous."

"Thanks Carol. I'm so glad you were able to get back in time."

"I wouldn't have missed this for anything. This almost makes me wish I were getting married again." Carol Smith and her ex-husband had one of the friendliest divorces Michelle had ever seen. They simply outgrew each other and because they had no children, agreed to an amicable dissolution of their marriage.

"Really?"

"Yes. I would consider getting married again if I found the right man."

"Any prospects?"

"No one special. Lately, though, I've begun to think how nice it would be to have someone waiting for me at home."

"I hear you, girl. I can't wait to go home to Michael."

"He's a good man."

"He sure is. God certainly has blessed me. But there's a good man out there for you, too." Michelle discretely pointed to Jeremiah Sanctuary. "What about him?"

Carol turned to where Michelle had pointed and saw a tall man, medium built, with salt and pepper hair and a full beard. "I don't know that man."

"But I do. He's the jeweler who designed my rings. Come on. Let me introduce you." Jeremiah was talking with Donavon when the women approached. Donavon smiled at Michelle and slipped his arm through hers. She smiled at him in return and spoke to Mr. Jeremiah. "I'm so glad you could attend our wedding."

"It's my pleasure, Michelle. I've known Michael since before he was born. He's like another son."

"And thank you for my beautiful rings. Michael told me the story behind them."

Jeremiah bowed his head slightly, but didn't respond.

"This is my friend Carol Smith," Michelle continued.

Jeremiah turned to the woman standing beside Michelle and smiled. "Jeremiah Sanctuary. It's nice to meet you."

"And this is Michael's father, Donavon Stephens."

"It's nice to meet you Ms. Smith." Donavon also smiled and Carol was thinking how attractive both of these men were.

"Same here, Mr. Stephens," Carol said, totally composed.

Michelle touched Carol on her arm. "I'm going to go talk to Aunt Shirley. I'll see you later, okay."

"I'll go with you," Donavon said.

"So, Ms. Smith, how do you know Michelle?" Jeremiah asked when they were alone.

"Carol, please." She noticed his gray eyes crinkled at the corners when he smiled and that he had obscenely long eyelashes. "I'm an independent contractor for her company."

"Oh, what do you do?"

"I'm a grant writer."

"That sounds interesting. Do you like grant writing, Carol?"

"Very much."

"I would imagine that a grant writer does a lot of research on a company before actually writing the grant, right?"

"Yes."

"So you must know a little bit about a lot of different things, right?"

"I've never thought of it like that, but I believe you're right," Carol laughed. "That makes me pretty smart, huh?"

"Sure does," Jeremiah smiled at her. "Now, the real question is, are you smart enough to have dinner with me one evening?"

"That depends," Carol playfully replied. "Are you smart enough to ask me?"

"Yes, my dear, I am."

"I'll have to check my schedule, but yes, I would enjoy having dinner with you. How do I get in touch with you?"

Jeremiah pulled a plain white card out of his inside breast pocket. "This has my home and cell phone numbers. Check your calendar and let me know. What kind of music do you like?"

"I enjoy most kinds, except bluegrass."

"The Three Mo Tenors will be in concert here in a couple of weeks. Would you be my guest?"

"I would like that, Mr. Sanctuary." Jeremiah raised his eyebrow, but didn't say anything. Carol knew what he was waiting for. "I would like that, Jeremiah," Carol amended.

Jeremiah smiled and said, "Why don't you give me your phone number and I'll call you in a few days to work out the details." Jeremiah took Carol's arm and began walking to the buffet table. "Let's get something to eat and we can talk more."

"I would love to Jeremiah, but you'll have to excuse me for just a moment. I'll be right back."

"Of course, my dear. I'll go get us something to drink and you can meet me at the buffet table." Jeremiah headed for the buffet table, poured two glasses of punch and bumped into someone as he turned to find seats.

"Oh, excuse me young lady. Are you all right?" The man speaking to her looked familiar, but Nikki didn't think she knew him.

"I'm fine."

"I didn't get any punch on you did I?"

"No, you missed me. It's okay."

"Are you sure? I would hate to have ruined your lovely outfit."

"I'm fine. Really."

"When is the baby due?"

"Excuse me!"

"Oh, I'm sorry."

"No, no. it's okay. You just surprised me. How did you know I was pregnant?"

"I saw you walking across the room. There's just something about the way a woman walks when she's pregnant. How far along are you?"

"Almost four months. Do you have children?"

"I have three, but two are deceased."

"I'm sorry."

"Thank you. By the way, I'm Jeremiah Sanctuary and you are...?"

"Nicole Peterson. It's nice to meet you."

"It's nice to meet you, too. Is your husband here?"

"I'm not married."

"Oh, I didn't mean to offend you."

"No offense taken," Nikki realized that she meant it. Mr. Sanctuary seemed like a nice man and she didn't think he was trying to offend her. There was something very familiar about him. Maybe it's his eyes. Or the beard, Nikki thought. Whatever it was made her feel an instant connection to him. "The baby's father doesn't know I'm pregnant" Nikki whispered.

"Have you tried to get in touch with him?"

"I don't know how. The phone number I had for him belongs to someone else." Nikki gasped out loud. "I am so sorry. I can't believe I'm telling a stranger my business, but you seem so familiar to me. We've never met have we?"

"No," Jeremiah laughed. "We just met a few moments ago, but it's not a problem," Jeremiah smiled down at her. "Nicole, do you know the Lord as your personal Savior?"

"I used to."

"Well, sometimes you have to trust that God has a way of working things out. We don't always know how, but He does. Will you trust Him with your situation?"

"I've tried to in the past. Some days it's easier than others."

"I know. I'm going to be praying for you. Do you mind?"

"No, of course not."

Jeremiah noticed Carol's return and motioned her over to where they were. "Do you two know each other?"

"Yes, we do. Hi, Nikki, how are you?"

"I'm fine, Carol. Long time no see," Nikki laughed.

Carol explained that they had just seen each other the day before at Michelle's shower. "The shower was fun. We'll have to get together when Michelle gets back."

"Sounds good. I'll talk to you later Carol. It was nice talking with you Mr. Jeremiah." She turned to leave, but Jeremiah gently took her arm and pulled her back. "Nicole, if you ever need to talk and I can be of service, please give me a call," and handed her his card.

"Why?"

"God told me to." Jeremiah kissed Nikki on the cheek and spoke directly into her ear. "God wants you to know that things are going to work out fine. Take care of yourself and the baby."

Nikki nodded her head again and walked away. Jeremiah turned back to Carol. "She's seems like a nice young lady."

"She is."

"Have you known her long?"

"Almost a year. She, Michelle, Sarah and I try to get together at least once a month."

"Girls' night out, huh?"

"It's really more like girls' night in. We order pizza, watch movies and catch up with what's going on with each other. You know, just a chance to let our hair down."

"Everybody needs somebody they can just be themselves with."

"Yes, indeed." Carol smiled up at Jeremiah and said, "So tell me about you..."

CHAPTER THIRTY-EIGHT

"Michelle! Who is that man talking to Carol?" Nikki anxiously asked.

"Jeremiah Sanctuary. He designed my rings."

"But who is he?" Nikki asked again.

"What do you mean?"

"There's something about him that seems so familiar, but I know I don't know him."

"Don't feel bad. He's just like that. Everybody feels like they know Mr. Jeremiah."

"No, it's more than that. Oh, never mind. You've got other things on your mind, right now. Like the wedding night."

"Girl, I can't wait. It's been a tough few months. There were so many times we wanted to give into temptation, but God helped us stay strong."

"I admire you and Michael for that. I don't know if I would have been able to do it."

"You would be surprised what you can do if you let the Lord help you."

"Yeah, so I've been told."

CHAPTER THIRTY-NINE

David still couldn't get over his reaction to Sarah. He had tried being patient. He had tried to give her space. He had tried to keep his emotions under control, but seeing her in that red dress was more than he could stand. She looked so beautiful, almost angelic. David prided himself on not being envious of much; however, watching his best friend marry the love of his life made David jealous. He wanted the same type of relationship with Sarah. She managed to avoid him after the ceremony, dropping his arm like it was a hot poker when they walked up the aisle. He was going to have to do something before he went crazy. Maybe they could find a quiet place to talk. Lord knows this house is big enough, David reasoned. Before he could go look for her, someone tapped him on the shoulder. He turned to find the woman he had been thinking about.

"Uh, David, I was wondering if...uh...." Sarah's nerves faltered.

"If what?" David prompted.

Sarah reminded herself to breathe. This was David, not some stranger. She could do this. "I was wondering if you would like to come over for dinner next week."

"Sure. When?"

"Thursday night. Around seven?"

"Okay. Who else will be there?"

Oh, no, Sarah thought, he thinks we're having a committee meeting. "Uh, no one."

"Excuse me?" David said in surprise. His hearing must be failing because it sounded like Sarah had just invited him to dinner without anyone else acting as a buffer. Maybe he had heard her wrong.

"It will just be you and me. For dinner."

David looked at Sarah for a moment and then burst into a huge grin. "Does this mean what I think it means?"

"I don't know," Sarah hedged. "What do you think it means?"

"That we can begin to explore what's between us."

"There's not..."

"Shush," David said as he put his fingers over her lips. "Don't say it. You know as well as I do that there's something, but we've been reluctant to find out what it is."

"I don't want to hurt our friendship."

"Sarah, the last thing I want is to hurt you. I like having you as a friend. But we can have something more. And I think you know that, don't you?"

Sarah nodded her head but didn't respond.

"This is what we'll do. We'll start with dinner next week and take things slow. We won't try to rush God or make anything happen. We'll just let it unfold according to God's plan and His will. Agreed?"

"Agreed."

"Good." David smiled and winked. "Now since you're cooking, I want some fried chicken, sweet potatoes and mustard greens. You know I'm still growing."

Sarah rolled her eyes. "Some things never change."

CHAPTER FORTY

Michelle was enjoying a few moments of solitude as she waited for Michael to return with a glass of punch. This was without a doubt the happiest day of her life. She was married to the man of her dreams and was surrounded by her close friends and family. She was looking forward to beginning her new life as Mrs. Gregory Michael Stephens, and wanted everybody to be as happy and blessed as she felt at this moment.

Michelle noticed Miss Julia talking with Michael's father and smiled to herself. They looked good together. Donavon was tall like his son and Miss Julia stood close to six feet. Michelle knew that she had never married and that Mr. Stephens, or Dad as he had invited her to call him, had been widowed almost thirteen years. Michelle had been praying that God would bring a good man into Miss Julia's life. Wouldn't it be something if God decided Donavon was that man? Michelle committed on the spot to stepping up her prayers.

Looking to their left, Michelle saw Carol with Mr. Jeremiah. Hmm, Michelle thought, they make a nice looking couple, too. Michelle figured they were about the same age, give or take a few years. According to Michael, Mr. Jeremiah had been widowed longer than his father and Michelle knew that Carol has been divorced for a long time. Hadn't she just said she was looking for a good man? Who knew what could happen? Michelle mentally added their names to her prayer list.

David and Sarah stood talking just to the right of Miss Julia and Dad. What is going on with those two? Michelle wondered. She knew that Sarah was attracted to David and she also knew he wouldn't make a move unless he was sure it would be accepted. She'd have to talk to Michael about this and see what they could do to get those two together.

Michelle saw her aunt and uncle cuddled in the corner. They were in their seventies and it was clear romance and passion was still very much alive in their marriage. Michelle prayed that God would give her and Michael that kind of love and longevity.

Brianna, Calvin and their kids were standing by the buffet line. The kids were well behaved stair-steps ages nine, ten and eleven. Michelle was looking forward to getting to know and spoiling her new niece and nephews.

Maria, Peter, Stephanie and Darryl were sitting at a table laughing. Stephanie's husband, Darryl, could have easily made a living as a stand-up comic. He had probably just told one of his jokes. Michelle realized she was surrounded by people who had successful marriages. Maria and Peter had been married twelve years; Stephanie and Darryl had been married fourteen.

Standing directly in Michelle's line of vision was her friend Nikki who was talking to Pastor and Lady Hooper. When Michelle got saved most of her friends fell by the wayside, but she and Nikki had remained friends, although they occasionally had intense discussions about religion. Michelle asked Nikki to be in the wedding, but she declined. The coral colored dress and duster hid her pregnancy beautifully. Michelle knew that the next few months and upcoming years were going to be challenging and she vowed to do what she could to help Nikki get through them. After all she and Michael were the baby's godparents.

Michelle saw Michael walking toward her and felt her stomach flutter. In less than an hour they would share a wedding bed. They had made a commitment to keep their relationship pure which had resulted in a lot of frustration. The wait would be over tonight. Michael had already given her a preview of what she could expect when he kissed her at the end of the ceremony. When Pastor Hooper gave Michael permission to salute his bride, he took the reigns off. Wow! If he had kissed her like that while they were courting, there would have been no way that they wouldn't have made love. But now, just like his letter said, he was free to give way to his passion. Michelle just hoped she didn't make a fool of herself and rip his clothes off!

Michelle smiled as she accepted the crystal flute from Michael's hand. He bent down to kiss her neck. "What are you smiling about?"

"I'm just imagining our friends being as happy as I am right now."

"Umm." Michael continued nuzzling Michelle's neck.

"And about what we'll be doing in just a little while," Michelle whispered in his ear.

Michael stood up, grabbed Michelle's hand and practically yanked her from the chair, which caused her to giggle. "Ladies and gentlemen, can I have your attention, please," Michael all but shouted. Once the room quieted down Michael continued. "Michelle and I want to thank you for sharing this special day with us. We thank God for the family and friends He has given us." Michael glanced around the room. "We're getting ready to leave, but we want you to feel free to stay and enjoy the food and the music. Thank you again for coming. We love you."

They attempted to make their way toward the front door, but were constantly stopped with hugs, kisses and well wishes. David whispered in Michelle's ear, "Told you so," as she walked past him. All she could do was smile. David would forever be welcome in their home because he brought her and Michael back together.

Sitting in the back of the limousine, Michael winked at Michelle and flashed his dimples. "I'm glad we waited." Michael leaned toward Michelle to share in another toe-curling kiss.

"Uh-huh."

Michael kissed her again. "But I'm tired of waiting."

"Ditto." Then Michelle started laughing and Michael joined in.

CHAPTER FORTY-ONE

DECEMBER 10

Michael's heartbeat slowly returned to normal. Making love with his wife stimulated all of his senses. He had committed as a teenager to save himself for marriage and had limited experience. During the month between the time he proposed and getting married he had read all the books he could find and talked to both his father and his pastor. He knew in theory what making love was, but had been totally unprepared for the reality of two people coming together in physical unity. Yet, even with his limited experience he didn't believe Michelle was satisfied with their lovemaking. She had orgasms and willingly came into his arms, yet she never initiated the lovemaking and always seemed to be holding back. Michael hadn't found any books that dealt with this and he was too embarrassed to ask anyone about it. He asked God to show him what to do. He wanted Michelle to be as happy as he was.

Michael brushed the curls from Michelle's face and planted soft kisses around her mouth. "You turn me inside out woman."

Michelle moaned her approval. "You don't do too bad yourself."

"Really?"

"Yeah, really. Don't sound so surprised."

"I guess I am surprised."

"Why would you say that?"

"Because sometimes I get the feeling I'm not satisfying you."

"What? You always satisfy me, Michael. I love making love with you."

Michael pulled one of Michelle's curls and watched it spring back. "But you never initiate our lovemaking."

"And because of that you think I'm not satisfied?"

"That and the fact that sometimes I feel like you're holding back. You come close to really letting go and then it's almost as if you make yourself stop."

"Well excuse me for not acting like a slut," Michelle said as she tried to throw the covers off and get up. Michael gently caught her by both arms before she could leave the bed.

"Hold up, baby. Where did that come from?"

"Let me go, Michael."

"Not until we talk this out. Come on, Michelle, talk to me. What's going on? I have a right to know if I'm pleasing you. I don't want our lovemaking to be one sided. If I'm doing something wrong, I need you to tell me."

Michelle let Michael pull her back down into the bed. "What did I ever do to deserve you?" Michelle asked as she leaned in for a kiss.

"What's going on, Michelle. I may be inexperienced, but I know I'm not wrong about you holding back, am I?"

"No."

"Why?"

"Because I don't want you to think I'm a slut."

"Why would I think that? You're my wife, my lover, my love. I know you're not a loose woman."

"But I used to be," Michelle buried her face in Michael's neck. "I wish I had been a virgin. I feel like I cheated you."

"Ah, sweetie," Michael softly kissed his wife. "I knew you had experience and I settled all that before I asked you to marry me."

"I don't want you to think I'm trying to throw my past in your face."

"Listen baby," Michael settled on top of Michelle. "If the roles were reversed and I brought my experience to the bed to make our lovemaking better, what would you say?"

"Hallelujah!"

"I know that's right," Michael chuckled. "But seriously, would you have thought I was throwing my experience in your face or would you just enjoy the encounters?"

"I would enjoy the encounters."

"Exactly. Baby, I don't hold anything against you. The past is the past."

"You sure?"

"Sure am. Beside, it's not as if I'm going to run into one of your old boyfriends, right?"

"I hope not."

"So here's the deal. You give me all you've got and I'll do the same. Together we'll learn how to please each other and we won't worry about who knows more or where they learned it or any of that stuff."

"Okay."

"I'm very teachable," Michael said as he nuzzled Michelle's neck. "Matter of fact, I do believe class is just about ready to be called into session."

CHAPTER FORTY-TWO

JANUARY 1—EARLY MORNING

Michelle woke from a deep sleep, stretched and tried to make sense out of all that she had dreamed about. Or at least she thought it was a dream, but some of it seemed so real. "Wow, God, I haven't thought of that stuff in years."

I know and that is part of the problem.

"What do you mean?"

Your repressed memories have made you unhappy.

"Yes, Lord, I know. I should be the happiest woman alive. I have a wonderful husband who loves and cares for me. I have a successful business. I have good friends, but sometimes I wonder what's wrong with me. I can't keep going on like this."

What are you willing to do about it?

"Whatever it takes."

Really?

"Yes, Lord. Whatever it takes. I'm ready to move on, but I'm stuck and I don't know where."

Yes you do. Are you ready to forgive those who have hurt you?

"Yes, Lord."

The man who raped you?

"Yes, Lord. I forgave him years ago."

All the men you had sexual encounters with before your husband?

"I don't want to think about how I used to act. Besides, that's under the blood."

You are right. I forgave you when you accepted my Son. But you have not forgiven yourself or them. Are you ready to do that?

"Are you going to help me?"

You don't have to go through anything alone unless you choose to.

"Then yes, Lord. I'm ready to forgive everyone who's hurt me."

What about your mother?

"My mother? What are you talking about? She was my best friend. I didn't have any problems with her."

Have you forgiven her for dying and leaving you with your father?

"Oh, my Lord!" Michelle exclaimed. She knew God was right, of course. She had been angry with her mother for dying and had often thought that it should have been her father. "Yes God. I'm finally ready to release that hurt and anger. Please forgive me."

You are forgiven. What about your father?

"I don't know about that one, God. That's asking a lot. If it weren't for him rejecting me, I wouldn't have slept around looking for affection..."

That is not his fault. Those are choices you made.

"Yeah, but, he could have loved me."

He loved you the best he could.

"It wasn't good enough."

No it was not, but that was not your fault. There was nothing you could have done. You tried everything you knew and it was not enough because you cannot control other people.

"I wish I had known that back then."

Everything comes in due time.

"Lord, please forgive me for all those wasted years. Years spent running from relationship to relationship, drinking, partying and abusing my body. My life had become a cliché and I didn't even know it."

I have already forgiven you for all of that. Are you ready to forgive your father?

"Yes Lord. I release all of the memories, hurt and pain of the past. I realize I've been holding onto the pain to keep people at a distance. I don't want to do that anymore."

Good, child. Now what about Michael?

"What about him? I love Michael very much."

I know you do, but he is one of those you keep at a distance.

"That can't be true, Lord. We're very close. I love him."

Suppose someone gave you a beautiful sweater and instead of wearing it, you kept it in the box, looked at it every day, but never put it to full use. That is how you treat Michael. I gave him to you as a gift, and instead of taking full advantage of the gift you are still in the looking-at-the-sweater-in-the box stage. You have not emotionally accepted your husband. You are holding back from him and depriving him of the wife he needs and deserves.

"How can you say that, Lord? I love Michael!"

I know you do. If you would take the chains off your emotions, that love would grow deeper than you could possibly imagine.

"I'm not sure I can do that. I've held things in for so long. I wouldn't even know how to begin to open up."

Trust him.

"I do trust him."

Trust him more. And trust Me. I gave him to you. You are safe with him, Michelle. He is not going to hurt you or abandon you.

Abandonment. That was Michelle's real issue. She had been abandoned by all the men she ever opened her heart to. Her father had been emotionally withdrawn. Brian had took her naivety and trampled on her feelings. And even Michael hadn't kept his word. He was the first man she really talked to after the rape. He told her he would call and didn't. Granted that wasn't his fault, but still it was a long time before she heard from him. What if he left her again? Was she willing to put everything on the line emotionally without some sort of guarantee?

"How can I be sure?"

You cannot. That is why you have to trust me. I know what is best for you, but the choice is yours. You can keep things the way they are and you will have a good marriage. Or you can let me help you and experience a great marriage.

"What if I can't? Are you going to be mad? I couldn't stand that, Lord."

Not mad, but disappointed. I am always disappointed when my children will not accept the gifts I offer.

"I do love you Lord."

I know you do, child. It will be all right. Just trust me.

"Okay."

Are you ready to forgive yourself?

"How can I do that?"

By accepting the love I have given you. By recognizing that you are a unique and valued creature. By stepping out of your comfort zone and realizing that no one is out to hurt you. By trusting me to fight your battles.

"That sounds like something my husband would say."

Yes, I know. Now, let me show you what I have for you to do.

CHAPTER FORTY-THREE

NEW YEAR'S DAY—MID-MORNING

Michael let himself in through the garage door and went looking for his wife. He found her sound asleep on the chaise and wondered why she wasn't in bed. He could tell by the covers that she obviously had been at some point. He hated having missed their first New Year's Eve together, but he knew that God had done something special for her.

Michael watched Michelle sleep and was once again struck by how physically beautiful she is; yet, he knew it was her inner beauty that really drew him. Michael smiled when he noticed her braided hair. He knelt down beside the chaise and gently stroked her cheek, covering her face with soft kisses. "Wake up baby."

"Michael. You're home."

"Yeah, sugar." Michael kissed Michelle full on the mouth.

"How did you get here? Were you able to get the truck fixed?" Michelle hugged Michael.

"You're not going to believe this," Michael said as he returned Michelle's hug. "This morning when I went to the lobby to ask about a tow truck or rental car, Uncle Jerry was there checking out. He had gotten caught in the storm, too, and decided to spend the night at the same hotel. When I told him what happened, he offered me a ride. It seems he's been coming to Columbus a lot lately to see Carol."

"I saw them talking at the wedding. There seems to be a lot of chemistry between them." Michelle was glad that her matchmaking abilities were on target. "He's a nice man."

"Uh-huh." Michael began unbraiding Michelle's hair.

"Why aren't you in bed?"

"It's a long story. I started in the bed and somehow ended up here. I don't even remember getting out of bed."

"It must have been some night."

"It certainly was," Michelle said and then burst into tears.

"Baby, why are you crying?"

"Because I love you."

"And that's something to cry about?"

"Of course not." Michelle tried to get a handle on her emotions. "But I do love you."

"I love you, too." Easing himself onto the chaise with Michelle, Michael drew her into his arm and placed her head upon his shoulder. "So why are you crying?"

"I got a hug from Daddy."

"Daddy?"

"Yes, Daddy God." Michelle gave Michael the brightest smile he had ever seen. "Let me tell you what happened."

Dear Reader,

The relationship between parent and child isn't always easy. If you are blessed with a father like Michael's, you are fortunate indeed. If, on the other hand, your father is more like Michelle's, you don't have to dwell on what could have, would have or should have been. God is the ultimate Father and if you will let Him, He can and will replace hurt, pain, grief and sorrow. All you have to do is trust Him. God alone—not positions, power or possessions—is what will get you through life's challenges. The Scripture writer was correct: It is in Him that we live, move and have our being.

A Hug from Daddy is a work of fiction with characters created from my imagination. I fell in love with all of them and I hope you did, too. I've often wondered how parents of multiple children handled diverse personalities and now I know! Michael, Michelle, David, Sarah, Julia, Jeremiah, Donavon, Amari, Carol and Nikki and all the others took on a life of their own. David spoke the loudest and insisted that his story be told next and I agreed. Book two—*The Wonder of Love*—is David and Sarah's story, and I can't wait to share it with you.

Although *A Hug from Daddy* is fictional, the transforming power of Jesus Christ is very real. If you haven't given Him your life, there's no better time to do so than right now. Just pray this prayer out loud:

> Father, please forgive me for all the times I've tried to do things my way instead of yours. I confess that I am a sinner and I cannot save myself. I believe that Jesus Christ is your Son who died on the cross in my place. I believe that He rose on the third day and ascended into heaven where He sits at your right hand. I believe He is coming back again. Please come into my heart and cleanse me from all sin and unrighteousness. From this day forward I belong to you, and I accept you as my Lord and Savior. In Jesus' name. Amen.

Once you've sincerely prayed this, you're saved. Now you'll need to find a church where the Bible is being taught and preached, and start telling everybody you know what the Lord has done for you.

The Lord bless you and keep you
The Lord make His face to shine upon you
And be gracious to you
The Lord lift up His countenance upon you
And give you peace

Numbers 6:24-26 NKJV

I would love to hear from you. Please e-mail me at obierogers@aol.com or visit my web site: www.obierogers.com to see what's new.

Please enjoy this excerpt from *The Wonder of Love*, Book Two of the Heaven on Earth Trilogy. ISBN 978-1-4495628-9-2

Sarah Caldwell, Ph.D., college professor, articulate woman of influence and mighty woman of God was running out of time. Her bedroom looked as if a fashion hurricane had run rampant. Silks, chiffons, cottons and wools in a rainbow of colors covered every available inch of space; typical of a woman trying to find that one special outfit for a first date.

Sarah sat cross-legged on the floor and blew out a frustrated breath. She had been trying on clothes for the past forty-five minutes and was irritated. "God, this is everything I own. I know that somewhere in this room is the perfect outfit for me to wear. I need you to help me find it, please." Everyone has their own way of working through problems. Some hummed wordless melodies, some doodled; others bit their nails, sucked their fingers or played with their hair. Sarah talked out loud.

"Concentrate girl, you can do this." She still couldn't believe her boldness in inviting David to dinner, and she had been a nervous wreck for almost a week. Now here she was minutes from being with him. She was shampooed, showered, perfumed and sitting on the floor in her underwear! "Get a grip and think this through. You don't want to wear anything sleeveless because it's November and you'll be cold. The fireplace will be lit so you don't want anything that's going to make you too hot. You don't want to wear a skirt, because you don't want David staring at your legs. You're nervous enough so don't go there. That leaves pants."

Sarah sat quietly for a few more moments and then gracefully rose from the floor and went to the chair where she had thrown several pairs of pants. She pulled out a black pair and then went to the foot of the bed where she had laid several sweaters. She chose a sweater set in magenta that she hadn't worn before and slipped it on. She went to the bathroom and applied lip gloss and mascara, fluffed up her short curls and exited the room. She stopped long enough to admire herself in the full-length hall mirror and liked what she saw.

She left the bedroom and went to check on dinner. As requested, she had prepared fried chicken, candied sweet potatoes and mustard greens. She had also prepared made-from-scratch biscuits and pecan pie. She had inherited her mother and grandmother's cooking genes and was very comfortable in the kitchen.

Sarah glanced at her watch and noted she had almost three minutes before the doorbell would rang. David was always punctual. She glanced around the living area of her condo. There was nothing else to do: the table was set, dinner was ready and the fireplace was waiting to be lit. She went to her bedroom to slip on her shoes and the doorbell rang just as she walked back into the living room.

"Here we go." Sarah put a bright smile on her face and opened the door to her destiny.

Other Books by Obieray Rogers

Waiting for Boaz: Encouragement for women
desiring marriage God's Way
ISBN 978-0-9764022-1-3

On the Other Side of Yes:
Understanding the Power of Agreement
ISBN 978-14664224-1-6
Available November 2011

The Heaven on Earth Trilogy (fiction)

Book One—*A Hug From Daddy*
ISBN 978-0-9764022-2-0

Book Two—*The Wonder of Love*
ISBN 978-14495628-9-2

Book Three—*Kiss Yesterday Goodbye*
ISBN 978-14664224-1-4
Available February 2012

WWW.OBIEROGERS.COM
A fresh voice in
Christian fiction and inspiration.

www.ingramcontent.com/pod-product-compliance
Lightning Source LLC
Chambersburg PA
CBHW020246150626
46552CB00020B/477